Our readers are our best critics.

What they tell us about
the Hollywood Legwoman Mystery series:

" … really spellbinding … hard to put down … "

" … great story … writing was beautiful."

" … told not only a fascinating story, but the author's writing is a pleasure to read."

" … exciting … wonderful … so much fun … "

"Meredith Ogden is a really cool character."

" … the most striking feature … the writing was beautiful."

"Great read. Spellbinding. Entertaining."

"Such an adventure. And so well written."

Meredith Ogden
Hollywood Legwoman Mysteries
by Penny Pence Smith

*The Last Legwoman—
A Novel of Hollywood, Murder and Gossip*

Sunset West—Guns, Grit and Gossip

Shadow of the Wave—Stranded and Stalked

Detective in the Crosshairs—Murder in the Desert

Also by Penny Pence Smith

*Under a Maui Sun
Reflections of Kauai*

THE FAT LADY SINGS

NINE STORIES FROM THE HOLLYWOOD BEAT

A MEREDITH OGDEN HOLLYWOOD LEGWOMAN MYSTERY

PENNY PENCE SMITH

150 Hamakua Dr. #357
Kailua, HI 96734

ISBN: 978-1-7372084-6-4 (Ingram Print)
ISBN: 979-8-3037411-0-2 (KDP Print)
ISBN: 978-1-7372084-7-1 (EPUB)

Cover design: Cynthia Gunn
Author photograph: Malia Leinau Myers
Cover photo © Bailey Alexander
Interior photo © Ryan Ancil
Interior design and book production: Elizabeth Beeton

This collection is dedicated to those collaborators and imagineers who help Meredith in so many ways as she forges the streets, far reaching streams and sorties of Hollywood. She's so much more because of them…

Nancy Vincler, Jim Vincler, Deborah Baker, Butch Wilson, Barbara Wilson, Bev Lenihan, Trish Roth, Susan Wagner, And Dixon Smith.

Meredith Ogden's and author Penny Smith's family, friends and colleagues are sending heartfelt wishes, thoughts and prayers to the victims of the massive Los Angeles fires that broke out as this book was being published. The "legwoman" journalist and the author have spent much of their lives in the many neighborhoods and residential centers destroyed by the blazes and share the sadness and shock of the assault.

ACKNOWLEDGMENTS

In *The Fat Lady Sings*, Meredith Ogden's life morphs in unison with the 1990s media landscape that, itself, has morphed and shape-shifted as time has passed. By 1990, the big metropolitan newspapers from the 20th Century were already becoming slim shadows of their former selves, and today, social media has given us all the ability to be a Hollywood reporter. Every Legwoman book follows the peaks and valleys that came with the territory of a print journalist constantly striving to find a home for their articles amid the changing landscape of that time. Two stories reach back to Meredith's earliest days as a neophyte in the shoes (Fendi, at least) of a legwoman. The "Back in the Day" stories are included to show the actual 1970s colorful if not bizarre landscape of Hollywood journalism and publicity. Today finds a subtler and/or broader field, especially through social media.

During Meredith's investigative journey, her loved ones, friends, colleagues rode the same bumpy bus in pursuit of their own next stopover. In *The Fat Lady Sings*, we explore, in short stories, some of those ancillary characters whose lives are snagged by the journey. Helping Meredith plan the trip were Nancy and Jim Vincler and Deborah Baker. The tour guides along the way were Beverly Lenihan, Trish Roth, and Barbara and Butch Wilson. Eagle-eyed Susan Wagner validated the tickets, along with Dixon Smith who cannot help but see errant hyphens and spaces, offer one-liners and is the invaluable, much-cherished, team cheerleader. Meredith, Raymond, Cassie, Ito and the rest of the entourage thank you, the readers, for giving them the impetus for traveling the undulating route. It has brought us all—writer and characters—so much pleasure and satisfaction to be one with you as a story family.

MEREDITH'S STORIES

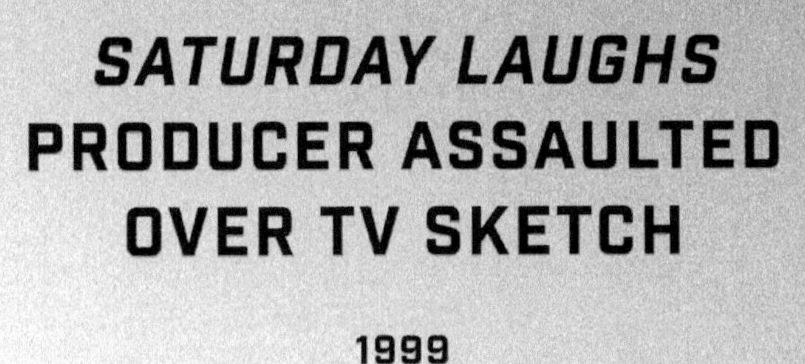

SATURDAY LAUGHS
PRODUCER ASSAULTED
OVER TV SKETCH

1999

1999
SATURDAY LAUGHS PRODUCER
ASSAULTED OVER TV SKETCH

It's the Weekend in L.A.!

Trudy Trubo opened the thick, carved wood door to the large house tucked solidly and comfortably amid the row of other Malibu Colony structures on California's legendary beach. Her smile was broad and welcoming, eyes flashing and sincere as she greeted Meredith with a quick hug and peck on the cheek.

"We are certainly flattered to welcome such a renowned journalist into our humble home," she crowed. Meredith returned the intimate "hello" gestures, amused at the moniker.

But then, Trudy glanced out to the street, suspicion and apprehension shadowing her gaze. She quickly closed the door behind her guest, securing double locks. Knowing there had been trouble at the studio for Trudy and husband, producer Bill Trubo, Meredith looked with question at the usually lively, open face of her friend. "Just being careful," shrugged Trudy. "We're currently in some cross hairs from irate non-fans, but since we also have a revered journalist in our midst and … well … caution and all."

"Yeah, I noticed the black and white cop car sitting at the curb," Meredith observed. "And by the way, this supposedly revered journalist looks more like a confused hippie," she said pivoting the subject. She glanced down at the tired Jefferson Airplane t-shirt she wore, cropped to just above a hastily chosen, swirling skirt of bright rainbow hues, nipping at her ankles. And athletic shoes. "Hardly 'revered' red carpet material! But I took a look at the sunny day and thought something frothy would feel good."

"Frothy. How boho!" mused Trudy. "Bohemian or just dowdy—neither of us will go down today as fashionistas!" Her open attractive face showed no make-up, brunette hair haphazardly secured in a large barrette at the back of her neck. She wore jeans, a Dodgers sweatshirt, and no shoes. The weight of caution and concern was still etched in her blue eyes.

The Trubos were neighbors whose beachside home was only a block and a half away from the house where Meredith resided with the special cases—entertainment industry focus—detective T.K. Raymond and their seven-year-old daughter Riley. The neighborhood was eclectic with well-appointed mini-mansions— like the Trubo's—residing next to nicely less opulent places—like Meredith and Raymond's. But the Trubos were also bona fide celebrities, who Meredith knew from her own travels throughout the world of show business. Bill was the originator and still producer of the two decades-long top-rated *Saturday Laughs* hit TV comedy show and Trudy, his long-time wife/lifetime partner and, once *Laughs* casting director, their early-twenties son away at law school, a teenage daughter, also absent—in college. Trubo had suggested he might retire at the end of the current season. Meredith's visit was to interview and chronicle the long and consistent yet changing focus of the show over its lengthy history.

As she entered the couple's casually elegant beach home, Meredith relished its subtly Asian influenced palate—not quite but almost a Japanese ambience and style of the room. The décor cast an air of serenity. As was her habit and manner after decades of exploring the inner and outer stories of celebrities, she looked for a deeper, more compelling story to tell than the obvious. Her "other" mission today was to talk to both Trubos about the troublesome audience reactions, sometimes menacing threats they received in response to the acerbic humor so celebrated on the TV screen. She knew there had been a death threat delivered to the studio aimed at

Trubo a few days prior, reaction to a specific skit on the show the week before. The incident inspired Meredith to call her friend and neighbor Trudy and request time to talk and gather information for a more robust column. The Trubos had worked with the journalist a few years earlier when their son had been detained in Iran as a "spy" and Meredith, along with one of NBS's top international field correspondents had partnered and worked with the family to report the family's story.

Sharing current family news, the two neighbors made their way into a room furnished in comfortable yet understated sofas and chairs. Warm, earth-toned inks and painted abstract art on every wall except for the one that was covered with Bill's awards: Emmys, citations and all the honors that come with highly celebrated innovation. Trudy gestured to a round worktable and excused herself to bring coffee for all. Meredith settled herself, set her bag on the table, pulling out her note tablet and pens. Bill Trubo, tall, slightly thick, his silver hair in need of a barber, entered the room energetically and approached Meredith with a wide grin.

"Welcome to the funny farm."

"How's your son Garrett?" Meredith asked. "All quiet after his episode in Iran a while ago?" Garrett had been doing graduate school anthropologic research in Iran and was captured and charged with spying. The incident was considered by most to be retribution for a comedy skit shown on his father's weekly show that parodied the current Iranian leader, Ali Khamenei. Bill Trubo shook his head and chuckled. "The folly is that my son's own youthful precociousness that cost us and the U.S. government so much angst and money to force negotiations and get him home … well, it made him a kind of celebrity." He shook his head with a cringe. "Probably helped him get into law school … " Trudy simply let out a sigh, returning with a tray holding a colorful coffee carafe, cups and a plate of small round cookies.

"I guess that episode was the most egregious criticism and retribution for one of your comedy skits, Bill," Meredith chuckled.

"I think you said then you wouldn't take on ANY Ayatollah again."

Bill shook his head and shuddered. "Had to work hard not to let that chill the normal creativity of the writers."

"But you must have a lot of folks you've parodied and featured over these years who've reacted by putting you and the show in the crosshairs?" The question stopped the conversation as Bill and Trudy looked at one another, understanding where the conversation would lead. The producer's face furrowed as he pondered the answer. Soon he began to recount some of the viewer blow-back the show's skits had taken over the decades. U.S. presidents the writers had lampooned, other celebrities parodied in satirical skits, popular trends ridiculed … . "Billy Wonder called us shit-heads. One U.S. press secretary said we were uneducated uninformed white trash. I'd like a dollar for every viewer-critic who's said we lie … "

"And yet they still watch the show … " Meredith murmured, jotting down Bill's comments. Her memory kicked in recalling so many of the edgy skits capturing and satirizing the cultural and political nuances of American life that made her laugh yet wince at the same time.

"Sure. But we don't go on air without a lot of review and evaluation by a lot of experts," he continued. "We are fully reviewed by the network legal department … Standards and Practices," he mused. "You should see what we don't air … "

"We also employ a staff attorney of our own," Trudy interjected. "Insurance," she added, bright but knowledgeable eyes tracking the conversation, also scanning the beach-side window with her on-going cautionary glances, clearly the threat from the studio resting heavily on her mind. Meredith, as well, wondered about the value of a police car on the street when the most accessible part of the house was oceanside.

"They all make sure we're not stepping over the lines considered acceptable by—well, the courts around the First Amendment, around the network's standards, generally acceptable public taste—all of it," Bill went on. "Most of the personalities we parody or target in our skits are already deemed 'public figures' which affects how they can be addressed openly, and there's a lot of legal background on the use of 'satire' which also provides leeway."

"It doesn't stop our adversaries from filing suits," Trudy interjected with a smirk. "They rarely get as far as court, but we do need the constant oversight and services of the legal beagles."

Meredith made notes and then looked at Bill. "What about you? When do you figure the level of taste or cultural acceptability has been over-stepped. And, do you step in to mitigate, or do you generally go with the writers' decisions?"

Trubo thought hard, deep furrows in his face. He shrugged. "Hard call, Meredith. I'm generations older than most of our writers—and the viewers we really want watching. I do step in, and I often negotiate. And I'm sometimes shocked at what actually gets aired in the skits." He paused and took a drink of his coffee. "I guess we need to back up—the real key is finding writers you can trust. To be innovative, creative, and yes, demanding and pushy. But also ones you can trust to have the good sense to know the difference between something so raunchy—or even trendy—that NO ONE could watch without grimacing—to something slightly or enough off-balance in today's world that would cause someone to wince a little but still laugh. And only a few would change the channel."

"What about the latest one—the threat that put the LAPD— among other law enforcement agencies on alert. Why I saw police cars stationed around the studio last week. And the one outside today."

Trubo rubbed a hand over his eyes, pinched his nose, thinking how to answer. Trudy looked out to sea. "Meredith, I can't talk in depth about it for all kinds of legal and security reasons," he spoke up. "But let's just say one should be careful taking on a devious newly minted leaders of a global ... er," he paused searching for a word, " ... let's just say menacing ... nation. The intelligence police from that team doesn't take well to sarcasm."

"You called one of those scalawags 'Rootin' Tootin' Putin' I believe," smiled Meredith. "And showed him with a posse of thugs dressed as cowboys. Then had them shoot up every day citizens who got in their way."

Trudy surreptitiously slid toward Meredith a blurry black and white photo of a figure using a public phone in one of the West L.A. malls. "Security camera—no real detail—but big accent obvious during the phone conversation." She chuckled. Meredith squinted to see the image of a solid, medium-build man, wearing a worn black leather jacket and a baseball cap shading his face.

Bill wagged a reproachful finger at Trudy. Meredith made a mental note to check out the last few episodes of the show for a better grasp on the story. She readjusted her position in the chair, mothering the long, clingy skirt. "Remind me why we used to wear these thinking they were so cool," she chuckled.

General conversation soon ebbed into the originally planned discussion, beginning with Meredith asking, "Bill, you've been the ringmaster of this humor parody for four decades, but this can't be the first time you've gotten barrages of dissention and threats. Your skits and actors are tough and relentless—politicians, celebrities, popular icons in all types of public situations … " And so, it continued. Meredith took notes, the chronology of the show and how it became a bastion of social criticism through humor unraveling as Trubo recounted it, story after story. After an hour, she stretched her neck back, flexed her fingers, then placed her pen and notes down.

"I read in *L.A. Home* that you have a legend-deserving bathroom with a great view. May I use it before the last three cups of coffee take their revenge?" Trudy escorted her to a set of modern, slender stairs and snickered, "Upstairs. Help yourself. It's a beautiful day and the view is sensational." Meredith mounted the steps and entered the wide earth-toned tiled lavatory. A jacuzzi and free-form open shower on one side, a long mirrored steel and granite vanity counter on the other, all framing a near-bedroom-sized walk-in closet at one end, a floor to ceiling window at the other. The bathroom's reputation was built around the window that overlooked the open ocean. "I'm not sure I'm deserving of this experience," Meredith mused as she viewed the place. Before re-entering the regular world, she washed her hands in one of the two giant clam-shell shaped basins. As she tweaked her ponytail she heard a hefty thud below. Turning off the faucet, she scowled, straining to listen as more softer thuds interrupted the usual quiet of the house. She heard what seemed a whimper, then a muffled scream and an unmistakable "pop." More clunking and then angry voices.

Tiptoeing to the still-closed door, she listened intently, realizing the door was designed as an ultra-modern sliding shoji screen and would make a noise no matter how carefully she slid it open. What she heard, regardless, froze both her spine and her thoughts—which zoomed erratically to the unmarked cop car watching the house and why it was there. Her mobile phone resting idly in her purse on the downstairs worktable, she twisted around to see if the Trubos had thought a phone in the bathroom necessary. Apparently not. None hung on the wall nor perched on a counter. Not her first episode where an intruder had entered the house and she was out of sight, Meredith knew violence was about to happen, if it had not already. She could hear voices—one louder, others intense. Another loud bark of pain. She glanced around, reviewing escape and rescue possibilities. While the window on the horizon offered unbroken seemingly open access to the outside, the room was actually well sealed with no other access possible. Except for the walk-in closet.

She silently moved across the floor, thankful for soft-soled athletic shoes, and made her way into the wardrobe-clogged space, elated to see it. And relieved to see a sliding screen door that made it accessible to and from the master bedroom. She gingerly placed her hands on the door—another modern shoji-designed panel. But as she carefully began to slide it open, she could already feel, sense, and almost hear the rattle it would make. She shook her head in frustration. Becoming ensnarled into the drama downstairs wasn't helpful to anyone. She had to remember that she had a young child of her own just down the street. And that her purse, ID, and notes, well identified, were sitting below on the coffee table. Hard to judge what the intruder would look at—for. She, too, felt vulnerable. She needed an escape route—for herself and for the Trubos.

Frantically gazing around the giant closet, she had a recollection of Trudy telling her once that the house originally was built decades before for an L.A. Crime boss and boasted hidden entries, stairwells concealed behind innocent walls—allowing an unnoticed exit should a threat arrive. She gingerly pawed through the rows of Trudy's dresses and slacks, blouses and jackets, under Bill's suits, chinos and jeans, becoming more frustrated by the second. She reached down to move a line of well-worn boots of many leathers to see a plain wooden panel the color of the wall but a more rough-hewn surface. Clawing her way upward behind the clothing that choked the side of the closet she saw the panel rose to the ceiling. She pushed but to no avail, tried it one more time on the other side of the panel and heard—mostly felt—a tenuous "click"—rusty but promising. The panel wobbled but did not open. She dug her nails into the seam between the panel and the wall and jerked, wincing at the strain on her fingers and her nails, willing it to budge—and silently. It did—only slightly—and with a whisper.

From below she continued to hear muffled but heated conversation. One voice obviously hyper and angered. She was more concerned by the previous "pop" and cry of pain. At least three minutes already passed, she figured. Five minutes could likely spell disaster for the Trubo family.

She frantically shouldered the row of clothing as far to one side as it would go, then wedged the door open—barely wide enough for her body to wriggle through hoping, at the same time, there was a working access at the bottom of the stairs so she could slip out. Hurriedly and half sliding—half butt-thumping—down the steep, gritty steps, pushing away spider webs, managing the voluminous skirt, she landed into piled up sand and debris at the bottom. Pushing herself off the floor, she realized that along the way her half-t-shirt had snagged on a nail or splinter, tearing the garment nearly off her torso.

Pulling at the fragmented shirt she realized just how dark the tunnel was and strained to what appeared to be a set of manual bolt latches securing the portal from outside intrusion. Working almost blindly, she forced open the three sticky mechanisms—amazed that they had not been replaced with more sophisticated, even technological, alternatives. But never mind. She slowly forced the door open and was out. Then suddenly realizing that to get to the closest—fastest—exit path from the beach, she would have to pass by the view from the ground floor window where the couple and their predator sat overlooking that portion of the beach. She nervously weighed the choice: the beach exit to the left, four houses and a long jaunt away—or the perilous exit next to the other side of the Trubo house. A quick jog. But any window observers would notice and wonder about the skirt, and the torn t-shirt barely dangling from one shoulder.

"Well," she shrugged, regarding the lank, now dirt-covered garments, "Bathing suits these days aren't much more than underwear with patterns. After all, it's 1999!" She stripped off the long fabric clinging to her legs leaving only her "French cut" panties covered in blue and white flowers, yanked off the torn, now soiled aged t-shirt revealing an exercise bra in bright blue, then pried off her shoes and, carrying them, took off running down the beach. Just one of many joggers on a sunny day. Nervous and avoiding a glance as she passed the window where the Trubos sat watching, she headed out a beach access path and across the street to the black and white cop car surveilling the house, advertised to be vigilant against any intruders.

Within minutes—after shouted instructions to call in back-up and a gasped description of the scene in the house—two more police cars snugged into Trubo's neighbor's driveway. Operatives from the security company monitoring the alarm system which had not been activated—were on their way. Meredith's heart beat so fast in worry about the Trubos she could hear the thumps in her ears as she checked the amount of time that had passed since the intrusion by the gunman—the escalating anger in his voice and what the result might be. As she sketched out a rough outline of the Trubo house, indicating the hidden stairwell, a shiny-faced young, uniformed cop scolded her. "Leave the premises now, ma'am," he commanded, turning a slight shade of red after noticing her running gear and redirecting his eyes to her face.

She regarded him with disdain.

"She's fine," commanded a gruff, deep voice. Meredith looked up to see the doughy countenance and exploding brush of grey hair of Don Sylvan, a veteran detective she'd met through her detective husband, T.K. Raymond, several times. The rookie glanced subtly at her panties, shrugged, and walked away. She handed over a rough-drawn floorplan she'd sketched on the back of a fast food flyer as another officer made a call to the Trubo's phone. No one answered. Soon his voice blared from a bull horn with a request to pick up the phone, a summons to exit the house and follow-on similar requests. The street was quickly shut down to passing vehicles. Meredith wrapped her arms around herself and gritted her teeth, grateful for her own escape but miserably conflicted by worry for her friends. And remembering the "pop" of a gunshot, the screams and cries of pain as she fought to stay focused on the current goings-on.

"Go home," said the thick, staunchly built Detective Sylvan, knowing she lived only a short walk away. "Good idea to put some pants on. T.K. will probably be here soon." Meredith winced realizing that Raymond's coveted but rare weekend golf game would—again—be interrupted by an altercation in which she was involved. And that he would probably shudder at her choice of wardrobe—or lack of it.

With her car stuck in the Trubos driveaway for the time being, she heeded the instructions and jogged down the street toward home—in spite of feeling heavy guilt in leaving her friends in danger but driven by concern for her own household.

Lupe, Meredith's steel-eyed grey-haired house helper stood on the small front entrance to the Ogden-Raymond front door squinting at the melee a block and a half away. Other neighbors were doing the same. As Meredith jogged up to the steps, glancing back at the gaggle of drama down the block, the older woman, hands on her solid wide hips, scowled and asked, "Where are your clothes?"

"Where's Riley?" Meredith barked, ignoring the question, pushing past Lupe—whose burnished cocoa face unfurled from scowl to surprise.

"In her room doing her reading," she sputtered. Meredith rushed into the house and ran up the stairs to the bedroom to put on more clothes. Pulling on jeans and a sweater, she detoured into the bedroom haven where her seven-year-old daughter was folded over her desk and a notebook.

"You okay, mom?" the youngster asked, startled, looking up from her work. Her tousled chestnut colored hair fell over her brow, golden brown eyes wide. Meredith nodded and affirmed all was fine.

"But close your window and the drapes—there's some trouble down the street. If you hear anything bad downstairs, lock your door."

"Trouble. Huh. Something you're involved in, again? "Mischief etched itself across the girl's face. She was the offspring of two heat-seekers, one a crime investigator, the other an inveterate reporter, both constantly embroiled in one or another mystery, drama or conflict.

Meredith smiled, threw her a kiss and had the errant thought that Riley already sounded like her dad. By the time the thought cleared her mind she was directing Lupe to stay indoors, close all the entrances and lock up. The house helper was still standing on the front stoop staring down the street as Meredith nudged past her, issuing the mandate.

"Something's happened down there. More people and lots of noise," Lupe reported as she slipped inside the door. Meredith heard the lock click as she pushed off the front steps into a run, pushed forward by worries of the Trubos.

In the scant fifteen minutes it had taken to run home and back, the situation around the Trubo house had changed drastically. A chittering throng of people now surrounded the house, but without pulsating tension or distress. Plenty of focus and noisy interaction. Don, the lead detective standing out in his bigness and his sagebrush hair, was huddled with the Trubos—sitting on the back of an ambulance, Bill holding what looked like an ice-pack on the side of his head, Trudy's hands clasped in her lap intently conversing. Meredith jogged to the trio, panting slightly, and gasped, "what happened?" Three sets of eyes turned to her.

"We had an intruder—a serious one with intent to silence the 'phonies on *Saturday Laughs*,'" said Bill, his voice tempered and sounding weary. "Came in from the beach. Stupid of us—didn't think to have security on that side of the house. Don't know how you heard him, what you imagined, or how you managed to sneak out—but whatever you did brought the law and saved our lives."

"I thought I heard a gun's 'pop,'" Meredith explained, settling herself on the edge of a cart sitting next to the ambulance.

Trubo nodded. "So jacked up he hit the wall instead, but it could just have easily been us. Probably soon it would have been. Disoriented him so badly he smacked me with the gun instead." The producer lifted the ice pack to show a large red welt on his temple.

"Guy was a mess—really unfastened, wacko," Trudi added. "Same crazy who threatened the studio yesterday. But they couldn't find him. Called from a phone booth in a department store. He's in that police car over there." She pointed at a dark Crown Victoria parked across the street. Meredith saw a clearer version of the blurred photo of the figure from the mall camera. Gaunt, angular face, cheeks covered with a scruffy uneven beard not yet beyond a late-night shadow, deep scowled lines across the forehead, lingering resolve and anger in his eyes. His dark hair was cut into an clean buzz cut. His shoulders , cloaked in camouflage, broom stick straight—as though he was proud of his situation.

"Part of a super-disconnected fringe group, apparently strong believers in the emerging leadership's power over Russia. Up-and-comer Vladimir Putin seems to be their superhero, I think," snuffed Trubo.

Meredith scowled. "Vladimir Putin? He's just a blip on the Russo-politico map. Didn't he just join the leadership's club?"

"Yeah, but we lampooned him," Trubo sighed, pushing the cold press into his temple even harder. "He was an easy target. These officers … " he continued, nodding toward the gaggle of law officers talking noisily, going about their follow-up work, "came in surreptitiously, scared the shit out of the guy and just overtook him. But … hadn't been for the surprise, the shock … I think he would have killed us." Meredith bit her tongue and thought how easy it might have been to simply hide in the closet and wait for fate to take its course.

"We went in through the hidden stairwell you sketched for us," the large detective said. "Glad you left the door unlocked—gave us a unique advantage—mostly silent and arriving from upstairs really unexpectedly … "

"I couldn't help but leave the door unlocked—it only had internal locks. No way to close them from the outside. I was so worried." Conversation waned and no one spoke for a moment until Trudy said, "I liked the flowers on the—um, bathing suit?" Her eyes actually twinkled.

"Boho doesn't work well for sand-slogging," Meredith shrugged. "And I realized that in addition to a good in depth piece on you, Bill, there's an immediately breaking news story here … " she gestured around herself.

"Yeah," he snuffed. "Not a subtle under-wraps gig anymore."

"I hope you don't mind but I have to file a story right now … " she winced.

"Better you than most," he sighed. "I asked the detective to bring out your purse and notes … our friend in the car never saw or touched them." Officer Sylvan handed over her belongings. She smiled at Bill, kissed him on the cheek, waved at Trudy.

A dark colored BMW was pulling up to the curb a few cars away. Meredith glanced over and had the sinking reminder that Raymond's golf score would be partial again this week-end. And his mood equally as half-assed. Her tall firmly built husband climbed out of the car, adjusting his civilian polo shirt, running a hand quickly through his silver-streaked hair.

He walked over to the ambulance rear where the Trubos, Meredith and Detective Sylvan were congregated. "I understand you had some trouble," he spoke with sincere affability to Bill and Trudy. "Everything seems calm right now. In a minute you can tell me about it. I've already been asked to 'check in.'" He reached over and affectionately squeezed Meredith's shoulder. "You okay? Figured you'd come over to help calm things down … and catch a good story." Raymond obviously hadn't yet heard of her involvement in the crisis. He'd no doubt echo Riley's words, "Trouble—again?" He turned, motioning to Don Sylvan. "Let me talk with Don and I'll be right back."

Meredith looked at the Trubos who were smirking as Raymond and his colleague walked away. "You okay?" mimicked Bill.

"Thanks for coming over to calm us," whispered Trudy conspiratorially.

Meredith shook her head then put a finger to her lips and murmured, "Maybe don't mention I was running the beach in my underwear!" She left in a hurried breaking-news-jog to file her story on the *News-New York* wire. Another day in the life of a Hollywood journalist.

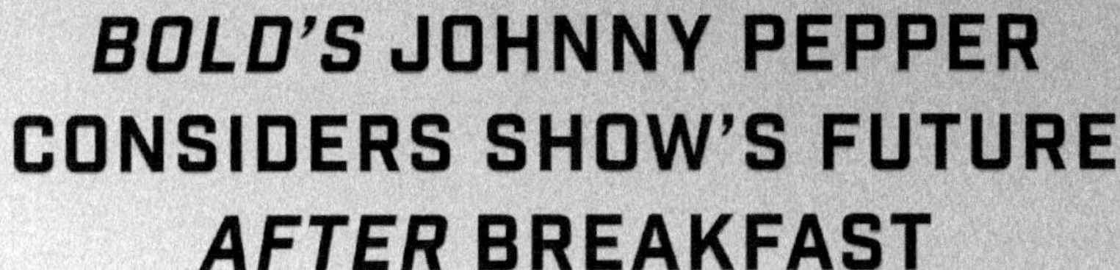

BOLD'S JOHNNY PEPPER CONSIDERS SHOW'S FUTURE *AFTER* BREAKFAST

1976

1976
BOLD'S JOHNNY PEPPER
CONSIDERS SHOW'S FUTURE
AFTER BREAKFAST

The Law Suit
A Meredith Ogden "Back in the Day" story

The slurried remainder of eggs, empty juice glasses and half used tabs of butter melting on crumb-laden plates were being scooped up by a well-seasoned waitress sporting a name tag that said Vera. The left-behinds of breakfast discarded into kitchen wash-bins, she returned to pour fresh coffee into the cups of the three diners who sat idly in the restaurant of the popular Sportsmen's Lodge, each looking bored and peeved.

"An hour late now," murmured Brent Osgood, a well-appointed silver-haired man, glancing at his watch. "Unbelievable." The head of publicity at CRC TV network, he was a rare participant at TV actor interviews. The other man, Bill Jolly, not-so-crisply attired but equally peeved was the chief national media publicity representative for Consolidated TV, a major production studio. The third diner was Meredith Ogden, whose by-line was the reason her breakfast partners were present to make certain her interview with actor Johnny Pepper went well. Other interviewers had occasionally veered off course with him with a less than positive published result. Pepper's weekly TV series, "Bold" needed a little positive pump to its audiences, and Ogden's reach and influence was why she was escorted by the studio honchos. They figured she was young, still polite in her stories, and probably a little awed by the presence of stars like Pepper. He had promised to talk about the exciting changes he saw for the series in the new season about to open. Fresh material made for good interviews.

So far—their TV hero had kept them waiting for an hour. The eight o'clock meeting time had been at his insistence. At half past the hour the dining room host had scurried over to tell the threesome that Mr. Pepper was running late but would see them soon. Now, a half-hour later, Meredith began to pull together her bag, notebook and prepare to leave. But swaggering through the tables headed their way, Johnny Pepper eyed them mischievously and yet with bold confidence, his sunlit hair a little disheveled, a lock hanging over his eyes.

"Hello," he said with a perfunctory smile, no extended hand, no acknowledgment of his own studio peers.

"Meredith Ogden," the journalist began but faltered as the actor slid into the open seat in the booth and snatched up the menu. There were no apologies, no casual greetings. He simply looked at the assemblage and said, "Please. I never talk before breakfast," then hailed the server, ordered a plain omelet and a grapefruit, with coffee. Then opened up a newspaper he'd carried under his arm and began to read.

"I'd like to move along," said Meredith, aware of the busy day facing her and the hour already wasted. Pepper looked at her, put a finger to his lips and said, "Sh-h."

"Why I sat there and waited, I don't really know," she later told her boss, gossip columnist Bettina Grant. "But when he did begin to converse, it was the dullest, least informative discussion possible. Nothing about the new season except what was in the media materials and a few confirming nods when I asked him about a story I'd read about him from an already published article. It was over in forty-five minutes. I left with a perfunctory 'thanks.' He nodded. Brent and Bill sat there looking like they'd each just swallowed a whole pickle. I'd love to know what was said when I was gone."

"Have fun with this one," Bettina said, puffing on her cigarette and turning back to her own work. "You can be honest, you know. Tell us the story you got." Meredith did. A rare young self-acknowledgment that she had the right and privilege—responsibility—to actually tell the story she got. It began:

" ... *Johnny Pepper was an hour late for our interview. He arrived dressed in a bright orange jumpsuit, dandruff sprinkles on his shoulder, hair askew, eyes puffy. To this reporter, he seemed like an aging movie star who'd been out late partying the night before ... Johnny says he doesn't speak before breakfast, so we waited another forty-five minutes to talk. And then ... "*

She had quoted his comments from other news stories he'd given recently. It only took about ten days before the phone rang. Meredith had expected some blowback from ... someone. Perhaps a perfunctory finger wagging from her studio and network contacts, a verbal chewing out from Johnny's own publicist or manager. She didn't anticipate the vehemence of the response she actually received.

Working at her own desk, pondering the schedule for the next few days, Meredith heard the droning conversation from Bettina's office where the columnist visited with an old friend, an actress who'd been on various TV series over the years.

Their assistant Sonia popped her head around the corner, eyes bulging, and told Meredith, "It's Brent Osgood—says it's important. Sounded serious." Meredith picked up the line.

"Meredith, I need to tell you something—but please know that all of us at CRC are in your court and will back you up—but Johnny Pepper is outraged and is threatening legal action over your story and is making a lot of other threats. Take a deep breath. Both Bill and I were there and can attest to what you wrote, but Johnny's a little out of control. Our VP of production is meeting with him later today." The network executive seemed to gasp at the end of his statement. Meredith felt a stab of icy fear in her brain and her gut. They were words no reporter—especially a young one—ever wanted to hear. She stammered to find a response.

"Brent," she began, reaching for her thoughts more than words, "he said nothing new or even interesting, so I quoted from other stories—I even credited them … "

"Meredith," her caller interrupted, "it's not about what he said or didn't say. It's really because you called him an 'aging movie star.' None of these actors can stomach that. 'Aging' isn't something most of them acknowledge."

"Yeah," sighed Meredith, realized the swat she'd delivered to the swaggering Johnny Pepper. "But Brent, I covered myself by saying, 'To this reporter, he seemed … ' I'm legally covered. It was my opinion and not said as a fact."

"It's not about any real culpability," Brent went on. "It's about retribution and anger and making your life miserable. He says he's sending letters to all of the editors who run your articles telling them you're a liar and a fraud and he never even met you. He named Kansas City, Boston, Baltimore, New York, Dallas … about ten editors. Your domestic big guys. But Meredith, they know you and your work so I wouldn't overreact. Let's see if he does it. But he also threatens to sue and even if he has no grounds, it'll be a shit show. I just want you to know. But also, that the studio will push back and convince him not to be foolish. It'll only make him look worse. I'm sorry that you had that experience. Sorry we all had to sit there and listen to his diatribe."

"Me, too," murmured Meredith. "What do you recommend I should do?"

"Sit tight and see what he does. Bill tells me Consolidated is taking the same stand. I'm guessing one or both of our companies will give him a legal opinion to let it go, just to keep the lid on this."

Meredith hung up shakily. She stared out the window, mouth dry, heart thumping. She didn't move for several minutes. Her fearful reverie was interrupted by Bettina Grant arriving in her office door. "I just got a call from Bill over at Consolidated. The columnist's face was serious and concerned. "Come on out here. Melanie Driscoll is here and has a suggestion."

The fitful reporter stood up, pulling herself to her full upright posture, determined to appear strong, and followed her boss to the living room of the home offices. A familiar attractive blonde—a "second string" TV staple—several series to her credit, never a starring role—sat comfortably in a wingback chair, pleasant looking and confident. "Hi Meredith, great to see you again," she beamed. Meredith smiled and found enough voice to respond.

"Now tell us what the hell is going on with Johnny," posited the actress, a bare hint of accent and her long-ago southern heritage peeking through. Bettina slumped back in her own chair and put a hand to her cheek. Meredith recounted the story and the threats.

"Well," Bettina began, "Bill said their lawyers are counseling Johnny to walk away. It's not his first negative story." She paused then started to chuckle. "Just the first one where anyone dared describe his behavior and his actual condition. But Merri," she used Meredith's youthful nickname now only used by a few very close friends. "The one way you can be sure to raise an actor's hackles is to call them 'aging.'" Her friend Melanie broke out in a loud guffaw.

"He deserves it," the actress snarked. Then sat up straight and looked at Meredith intensely. "Seriously, though. Call my husband, Jerry. He's a showbiz attorney and will have a different take on this." Meredith stomach seized. She'd hoped this little incident would go away. That she'd not have to deal with drama or serious problems. She shook her head and waved the thought away.

"The syndicate will also take a legal stand—they do that—if this whole thing should come that far," said Bettina. Meredith gulped silently again.

Back at her desk a while later, the attorney Jerry called her. "Look, Ms. Ogden. Melanie told me what happened. What a jerk. But, let him send the letters, make all the threats—your stock with your editors will go up much higher. AND, you can then sue him for all kinds of harassment, restraint of trade or a whole bunch of other things. Johnny's got very deep pockets. You could win big on this one."

Meredith felt her teeth clinch and the spine compress. They talked casually about possibilities for a short while, then she quickly clamped down. "Let's see how it plays out, Jerry, I'll call you if I need your help—but thanks so much. You've given me a lot to think about." Bettina stuck her head into the office and asked Meredith, "Are you doing okay?"

Meredith sighed, shrugged and said, "Yeah, I guess. Lots of opinions and perspectives. I think I'll go home and just try to let go of this."

"Good idea," laughed Bettina. "No matter how it plays out, it will be really good for you. Our editors will think even more of you as a true observer, commentator on the industry. And," she pointed at Meredith, "your writing is starting to hit with a closed fist instead of an open handed smack. Big difference. About time." Meredith could only shrug. Bettina bowed out as quickly as she had arrived.

A fast call quickly went out to Meredith's main male companion, Dusty Reed, five-foot-nine robust and brawny figure of a man—movie stunt professional with an affable, contagious demeanor, twinkling eyes and genuinely happy smile. "Can you come over tonight—maybe soon. I'm a little frightened to stay alone."

"What'd you do this time, Merri," he said with a slight chuckle. "Who's after you?" It was meant as a joke.

"Johnny Pepper." Silence.

"Oh. Well, he's a lot more bark than bite," Dusty finally spoke. "I've worked with him and he barks a lot. Growls a lot of the time. But I wouldn't say he's really just a pussy cat!" Dusty snarked. "What did you do to him to cause his ire?"

"Said he looked old and tired," answered a meek Meredith. She could almost hear Dusty wince at the other end of the line.

"I'm on set until about six," he said. "I'll be there after. Ribs tonight?" That meant he would pick up dinner from one of his favorite barbeque places that was near the studio where he was working. She agreed enthusiastically.

Dinner dishes and take home detritus cleaned up and in the trash, Meredith and Dusty curled together on the sofa in her west Los Angeles condominium watching the late news. "No trespassers or intruders," murmured Dusty. "I think it's safe to call it a night."

"Stay?" Meredith whispered.

"Duffle's in the Jeep."

Meredith shrugged awake often during the night at the slightest noise she didn't recognize. Dusty slept on giving her the security she needed. Paco, her cat, kept watch from atop the refrigerator. As they scurried around the kitchen the next morning, Dusty chewed on a piece of toast as he prepared to saddle the Jeep and head to work. "By the way, I have to work on Friday night. I can't go with you to that network thing."

"The reception for the new news director?

"I guess."

"I can hitch a ride with Fred. He uses his role as Hollywood's favorite trade publication editor-in-chief to fill his bachelor evenings with parties, and other show biz events. I do feel like I want someone stronger than me at my side. Johnny Pepper's show is on the same network and I'm sure Fred'll be going to the party."

"Rogue reporter," growled Dusty. "Meredith Ogden on the prowl—stronger than a Brillo pad!" She punched him in the arm as he kissed her lightly and headed out the door, the well-used back canvas duffle bag thumping against his shoulder.

A few days later, Meredith found herself at the reception for the network's newly arriving news director. "I was going to bring Ursula—the model from those lingerie commercials," Fred told her, offhandedly, while picking up a glass of wine from the tray passing by. "But she didn't feel well at the last minute. I'm glad you called." It was a familiar refrain from Fred Barton, gonzo Hollywood editor but insecure man, small and wiry in nature, but a dear friend and Meredith's former boss. They often made the rounds of show business social events, both with the clout to be treated with high attention and respect. It was a comfortable pairing for industry events. Although Fred always felt it necessary to remind everyone of his connection to luscious lovelies like the famed Ursula.

"Well, Fred, be on your most powerful best," Meredith snickered. "I need a bodyguard." He looked at her with wrinkled brow and quizzical gaze. "Johnny Pepper," she offered. "He didn't like my story."

"Hope you got a better interview than I did a while ago," Fred murmured, studying the golden liquid in his glass. "Poor choice of wine," he murmured. "Johnny … well, believes his own press releases. Thinks he's the hot bodied super guy he plays. Not. Not anymore, at least." Somehow the words should have been a comfort to Meredith. But she still worried.

A while later, Bettina Grant sashayed up to her as she perched on a short wall on the terrace outside the event room. "Not hiding, I hope," said the forthright columnist, her blondish-red hair tucked behind one ear, a mass of curls otherwise. She held an unlit cigarette in one hand, a glass of amber scotch in the other.

"I did catch a glimpse of Johnny Pepper a while ago," Meredith said. "It just felt safe out here."

"Damn," said Bettina. "Stop over-thinking this—or avoiding something that's bound to happen sometime, anyway. He'll be around for a long time and so will you. And, that guy's not gonna do anything but ignore you. He's more afraid of you than you should be of him."

"Said the lion trainer just before his charge ate the assistant." Meredith was, in fact, reassured by her boss's words.

"Hey—you're your own byline now," chastised the senior journalist. "You didn't interview Johnny as me. And you wrote about him from your own point of view. Meredith … " Bettina moved to stand in front of the younger woman, staring her in the face. "Fuck him. He can't beat you up or do anything but make himself look bad. Toughen up and take both credit—and responsibility—for your own power."

Meredith nodded meekly as two colleagues made their way

toward the duo and greeted them. Fred came to collect her soon after. She caught a glancing view of Johnny Pepper across the large event room as she exited the event with Fred at her side.

The next day, she recounted the whole story while relaxing around the pool at Meredith's condominium complex. Gloria Talmadge, the willowy brunette, former college roommate, long-time friend and newly minted Los Angeles attorney stretched out on the chaise lounge, scratched her head and puzzled, "What did you do that caused him such a reaction that left you forever paranoid about him?"

"I basically called him old."

"That'll do it," chuckled Gloria. "But what do you think he can do to you anyhow? Smack you around in front of people? Poison your drink? Worse, toss his in your face?"

"No," Meredith conceded, comfortable and secure in the company of an old family-like friend. "He could start yelling at me, berating me and calling me names—a liar and worse—in front of my peers. I interviewed his ex-wife a year or so ago. Didn't know she'd been married to Johnny. She said he could be totally distant, dismissive—self-absorbed—unless he got mad. Then sometimes exploded into nasty verbally abusive behavior toward her. Didn't care where he was or who was around. Really out of control, in her eyes. I'm really just getting to be an integral part of the professional media community and can't stand the idea of being lambasted publicly."

Gloria "tsked" and chuckled. "Guess who would win that reputational battle by standing tall and saying nothing?" She pointed at Meredith.

A month later at a studio premiere, Meredith lingered in a crowd of attendees when she realized Johnny Pepper stood next to her, almost touching her elbow. She froze and quickly turned away from him. But the assembled group surged toward the theater entrance and Pepper's eyes fell directly on her face. She frantically glanced away, moving in concert with the group around her. But

Johnny Pepper's face remained on hers—and never connected nor registered familiarity. She was a stranger to him. He glanced at a nearby news camera and went to join friends standing in its lens.

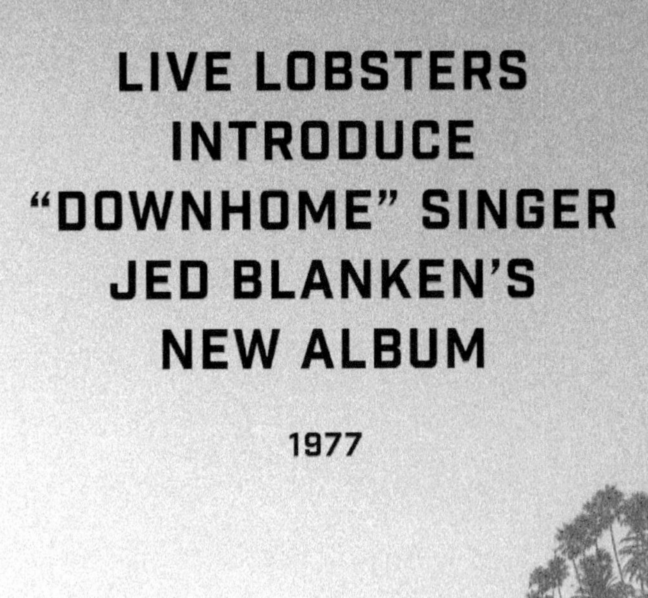

LIVE LOBSTERS
INTRODUCE
"DOWNHOME" SINGER
JED BLANKEN'S
NEW ALBUM

1977

1977
LIVE LOBSTERS INTRODUCE
"DOWNHOME" SINGER
JED BLANKEN'S NEW ALBUM

A Meredith Ogden "Back in the Day" story

"Mrs. Bettina, come quickly," demanded the strung-tight voice of the white-jacketed man who opened the door to a large, bright green portentous-looking cooler, left behind on the welcome mat without a delivery person in sight. Ito, the houseman at the residence of gossip columnist Bettina Grant, twitched nervously at the voracious scratching coming from within the strange parcel on the doorstep.

"Mrs. Bettina!" he called again. A nicely folded note sat atop the delivery.

Usually, when the doorbell rang on a Friday afternoon two weeks before Christmas, the small staff in the home office of gossip columnist Bettina Grant hardly noticed. A busy news office with daily national deadlines was accustomed to deliveries and special packages. And Hollywood news was especially like that, with studios, producers, singers, celebrities sending a holiday remembrance in hopes of quid pro quo when their next movie, record, or perhaps TV series arrived to the public.

Unfolding the note, Ito was confused by its content. The forthright young Japanese man was fluent in English, but the words weren't the problem.

Gossip columnist Bettina Grant came quickly to the door.

"Legwoman" or assistant, Meredith, and secretary, Sonia, followed close behind. They all bent over to the strange container, straining warily to hear its sounds.

Ito grabbed one end and struggled to drag it into the house. He grunted with is heaviness. Meredith moved to the other end and lifted it. Together they half-dragged, half-lifted it into the entrance hall. Bettina snatched up the note and read it aloud. "Happy holidays from Jed Blanken—all the way from Maine where he will be singing a Christmas concert on December 22nd, the release day for his newest song 'I'll give you a rosebud each morning.' Thought you would enjoy a taste of our famous, succulent Maine lobster while Jed sings his best wishes from the stages of his beautiful state."

"What the hell?" snorted Bettina. "Live lobsters—five of them." She groaned.

"Live lobsters as a music promotion?" muttered Sonia, shaking her head. "Ludicrous."

The entire group just stared at the Package. "On a Friday afternoon," Bettina whimpered. "We've had a lot of dizzy promotions sent to us, but nothing like this. These guys have to be cooked very soon or they'll spoil. Well, die then spoil."

Ito tore the tape from the container and lifted the top of the cooler only far enough to glimpse the wriggling, scratching crustaceans—also trying to make sense of their surroundings.

"Cook them?" squeaked Sonia. "No! We can't do that! They're alive!"

"We could toss them into the pool?" Meredith offered.

Bettina just shook her head in disbelief. "What idiot publicity person would do this?" She ran a hand through her "stay-in-the-office-day" fly-away hair. "The fact that Jed is from Maine can't really be the only thing they could promote."

Ito stooped down to peer more intently into the container. "Five of them—noisy," he reported.

"What are you supposed to write about this?" Sonia asked.

"They hope it's something about Jed's new album," Bettina

murmured.

"Broiled lobster—lobster Thermador—Lobster bisque—high priced at fancy restaurants," Meredith murmured. "You never notice that you have to boil them."

"Who does?" asked Sonia. Meredith nodded toward Bettina who pointed at the slight Japanese man wearing the white coat. He looked stricken. "So, in order to sell albums, this dude in New England wants people to kill lobsters?" The secretary tsk'd.

"Well, someone has to use these somehow," "Bettina pressed onward, sincerely. It would be a travesty to let them die in that container." No one spoke, mostly stared at the cooler.

"My Aunty Nico can help," Ito spoke up quietly. "She has been a chef and managed a restaurant. Maybe she can prepare the food and make it delicious." Relief greeted him from three faces.

Soon Ito was handed the keys to Bettina's beloved Jaguar. Driving it was one of his most cherished past-times. The group managed to heft the container into the back seat with Bettina continuing to forcefully warn, "Don't let that spill in my car!"

He drove off with no further suggestions or plans other than foisting the problem on his aging aunt a half hour away. The group went back to work still shaking off the amazement of the moment and situation. Maybe there would be a lobster dinner that night. And if so, were any of them willing to dine on the precious sea bounty that they'd come to know somewhat personally?

From her own office, Meredith discreetly called Jed's publicity representative, Cory Dailey. Cory worked for one of the entertainment industry's larger publicity firms. Maine resident and singer Jed Blanken was a client. Cory's job was to plan and carry out his promotional contact with the media that wrote about celebrities like Jed. "What were you thinking?" Meredith huffed.

"Well, sometimes," Cory's youthful voice said contritely, "the client—the celebrity—has his own ideas and isn't willing to change them. And he pays the bill."

Meredith grunted a vague acknowledgment of the dilemma,

then added, "Besides violating every PC rule with the animal rights organizations, how in the world do you—or Jed—expect most people to boil and serve these guys in an afternoon?"

A wistful sigh answered from the other end of the phone, "Yeah, we told Jed that food sent as a promo tool is always risky. Do you remember the asparagus folly?" asked Cory.

"No."

"Before your time, I think. But the producer of *Millie's Land*— that heartfelt happy farm girl series from a few years back—placed the series location on a wheat ranch in the Pacific Northwest. You can probably guess that the producer had a ranch of his own in the Pacific Northwest. Renting it to the studio was a very nice income generator.

"Well, his real-life ranch decided to start growing asparagus, a big very lucrative crop. And complicated to start. So, the producer incorporated the introduction of the new crop into the scripts of *Millie's Land.* And the publicity folks came up with this stupid idea to send beautifully crafted wooden boxes full of Grade A fresh asparagus—plus a recipe for a great asparagus dish—to key press and important sponsors of the series. When there was a slow-down in the mail delivery—don't remember why—all those packages of fresh asparagus sat in the back rooms of post offices throughout the country. And arrived badly spoiled and very odiferous."

"Ugh," snarked Meredith. "Well, if we can't figure out what to do with these unhappy lobsters soon, they'll have their own special odor."

"Maybe they should have their own TV series," chuckled Cory. The two commiserated for a few more minutes before closing the conversation off.

Three hours later, the Jaguar pulled into the garage. When the staff heard the electronic door open and close, they hustled to the side kitchen door to see what Ito and Aunty Nico had created.

Ito entered the house clutching a fat tub-sized salad bowl filled with a bounty of greens and vegetables. And, he escorted a diminutive grey-haired lady, slightly bent, with a huge smile on her face. "I'm Nico and dinner is ready," she crowed in a slightly accented voice. "Let's set the table."

As they did, Ito had returned to the garage and was extracting the rest of dinner from the Jag. He returned, juggling five large pizza boxes.

"We gave the lobsters to the aquarium—and picked up pizzas."

SILICON VALLEY MOGULS
OPEN NEW MOVIE STUDIO

1998

1998
SILICON VALLEY MOGULS
OPEN NEW MOVIE STUDIO

Chips and Sal's awakening

Slipping the stretchable white booties over her shoes and securing the hoodie around her face, Meredith Ogden wondered why a journalist covering a show business story was asked to don cleanroom scrubs to look at a technology lab that had no bearing on the story she was covering for the *News-New York* syndicate. The subject was the opening of the Silicon Valley's own major movie studio complex.

"You should understand the full scope of what we're trying to do here," her corporate escort told Meredith as he gave her a tour of the mother-ship facilities of one of the largest computer/ electronics tech companies in the world. And located in San Jose, the heartbeat of Northern California's Silicon Valley. "They're working on integrated circuits—ICs or chips—which are the electronic heart of all computerized products. The intelligence. Cars, appliances, media, and so on."

As the journalist peered around—she questioned, as well as felt, some concern—at the purpose of visiting the hive of workers draped in their sheet-like robes, hoodies, gloves and booties—like her own—hunched over instruments that gave Meredith no clue what-so-ever about what they were doing.

Meredith Ogden had arrived in the throbbing tech capital of the country only the evening before, checked into Hyatt Rickey's, the Valley's go-to hotel, with plans for a two-day-long stay to explore the combined industry's latest brainchild: a self-contained, stand-alone movie studio. Complete with all the technology bells and whistles—visuals/audio tools, near-galactic staging devices, administrative processes—to establish its own theme-focused entertainment complex. The themes: technology's past, present and future in glistening futuristic fiction, absorbing noir stories of the past, and colorfully imagined and dramatized mysteries and suppositions of what could actually be happening behind the veil of everyday tech development.

"The legends in the Valley still rule," snarked her project guide. "They're million-billion-aires, control most of the car engines, manufacturing machines, communications devices of the world. But in reality, the wunderkinds all just want to direct movies." Positing the rationale for the development taking place in the Milpitas area east of San Jose, on the apron of the San Francisco Bay, on land purchased by a consortium of the larger, more powerful Valley tech companies. Championed by three early pioneers, Jay Dillington, founder of Sanddabs Software, Bob Sands of Bearbite Machine Power and the grandfather of them all—Ivan Milsap of Fairweather Electronics.

Meredith Ogden, normally chasing movie, TV music Hollywood-type stories, had been invited to visit and was intrigued by the idea of a power grab by the very tech giants upon whom the film industry relied more and more every day. Her host was Rob Hatman, the Marketing Director of the Museum of Computers, Science and Technology in Cupertino. A former journalist and Valley PR professional, Hatman had been a college classmate of Meredith's at Northwestern University decades earlier. They'd stayed in contact over the years. Hatman always said she had the glamorous spotlight job, he the darkroom no-light one. Until the computer industry burst from the shadows becoming the "it" kid in the media.

"You still wear better clothes than I do," he complained. When he had contacted Meredith about coming up, at the industry association's expense and writing about the lofty studio plans for her world-wide syndication readers, he wheedled and threw out incentives. "You can share lunch with the most powerful tech giant in the world … you can stay in the suite Steve Jobs might have once used … you can see where the first computer was built … " But Meredith's incentive was that she'd heard through another former classmate, Lucy Gilman, now an editor and co-owner of a small twice-weekly paper in nearby Santa Cruz, that the tech industry power team was really hoping to build their own city, more like a state, where they could … well, anything they wanted. Meredith idly thought they already had done that on the Peninsula known as the Silicon Valley and the movie studio was one more building block. She also knew technology had been part and parcel of the cinema industry for a long time, but the studio idea was intriguing. And her hunger for unusual stories had suffered a shortage for a while. The idea of Hollywood-style activity in an entirely new frame was too good to pass up.

"But watch your back," her friend Lucy had cautioned. "It's not only predator city but is home to world-class slicksters who want to be—and often have you believing—they're the next Coming." Meredith pressed her for more, suspicious of the warning. "You're only in town for two days and nights just be careful what you ask and what you hear. Since I'll be visiting with you the third night, we can talk more in detail then." Her words etched themselves deeply into Meredith's psyche and they lingered in the back trails of her mind.

Meredith had launched her exploration of Hollywood in high tech on a Sunday evening, kissing goodbye to her stalwart and solid partner of a husband, detective T.K. Raymond, and their five year old offspring Riley. Leaving them in the hands of the house helper Lupe, her grey hair pulled into a haphazard bun at the neck, her curled fists often lodged firmly at her wide tank-like hips. The aunt of their previous long-time helper, Lola, who'd left after obtaining her master's degree, Raymond referred to Lupe as "El Générale." Meredith thanked God for her.

Day one in tech town for the journalist was a mandated visit to a development lab in the massive Fairweather Electronix headquarters. Fairweather's Ivan Milsap "father of modern electronics and computing," as host Rob Hatman had explained, "insists that newcomers see the level of intricacy and complexity involved. How the whole shebang we know as the computer era functions at the heartbeat level … " Meredith nodded and complied although she'd rather be touring the greater part of the San Francisco Bay Peninsula known as the Silicon Valley. Just to get a visual. Ivan Milsap had greeted Meredith and Rob with old-world dignity and charm. At 85, the iconic tycoon still played a key role in the massive company and insisted on personal courtesy wherever and whenever he was present.

"You'll have a private dinner tonight with Sanddabs' founder and CEO Jay Dillington and Mr. Milsap," Hatman had explained. "They'll tell you the full story of how this movie studio came about and why it's such a big deal to the industry. At least to the funders," he added with a ring of cynicism.

"I'll need some time this afternoon to read over the packet of information you've given me," Meredith said, looking at the thick slickly designed press folder. "Hope there isn't a test," she muttered.

"Today, is indoctrination day," Hatman answered in exagger–ated importance. "Tomorrow morning you'll have breakfast with Bob Sands from Bear Bite and, of course, Todd Salem, then we'll go to the site for the studio for the big groundbreaking with all the celebrities." Meredith could hear the mirth in his voice. Old friends didn't have to pretend.

"And who will be there?" she asked.

Hatman named a few actors, mostly TV names. "And, well obviously Todd Salem—he's the Hollywood partner/investor and the studio will carry his name. They felt an overall Hollywood name would gather more traction and media." Meredith snickered. Todd Salem had been the star and audience swashbuckler-hero of seven space fantasy movies that had become not only income winners for their time but set the stage and trend for an entire generation of movie themes for the next fifteen years. Salem had flirted with and become headline mates with the tech giants who, like most of the movie-going public, also besotted by the genre and Salem's macho presence. "There'll be separate sound stages named for the electronics guys—Dillington, Sands, Milsap and others as well."

"Who else are partner funders of this project?" she asked over lunch.

"Three other smaller—I could say 'lesser'—but I won't—stalwarts in the Valley electronics community, and one very large venture capital company. Frogner Venture Partners. Even the money guys want to be a part of Hollywood." Meredith snickered into her hand.

She'd hoped for a simple meal which she got—in what Hatman called "an industrial deli, a staple, he explained, of the tech world. "This one is now infamous—it was one of the first in the San Jose area—carved out of an extra warehouse space in a newly developing industrial complex with no other food services within five miles. They made it as close to an automat as possible—vending machines with sandwiches as well as snacks and drinks. But eventually a gourmet chef took it over and made it a 'go to' spot for the Valley. It still sported metal tables and chairs, paper plates and plastic utensils and vending coffee and drinks, hamburgers, etc. But a larger menu with "really good food." And expanded prices.

As they were leaving the deli, Rob continued the verbal agenda. "You'll have time alone with Todd tomorrow morning, of course." Of course, thought Meredith who'd had more interview time over the years with the actor than she cared to remember. Hatman then named off a small handful of other celebrity names, none so prominent as Todd Salem. After trekking through electronics clean room after clean room, lab after lab and "newest—state of the art" business centers and offices, one after another, a late informational lunch, she was glad to finally return to her room to peruse the materials and turn off the public persona.

She called Riley who was home after school by then. All was calm and stable in the life of the five-year-old who asked "Are you going to a fancy ball tonight?" Meredith laughed, realizing the youngster didn't quite know what to make of the idea of a dedication or groundbreaking or …

"Tonight, I'm just going to dinner with two very famous computer geniuses," she explained. "They started some of the computers you use at school and that dad and I work on. They own the new movie studio."

"Why?" asked the child. Meredith wondered the same thing but recalled—without repeating it—Rob Hartman's comment, "What they really want to do is direct movies."

☆☆☆

At five-thirty, from her overnight case, Meredith rescued her plain black travel dress with the low back and quietly form fitting lines. A simple sheath. An added jacket. Silver hoops on her ears and a simple but elegant silver necklace, low heels. All just a frame for her athletic figure, sculpted face, large brown eyes and still copper hair. At the front entrance to the verdant and retro hotel grounds she was escorted into a black limousine which took only about 10 minutes to the entrance to a different hostelry—one modern enough to merit its prominence in the world of space age technology. Walked through the starkly elegant lobby and modern techno-art-filled halls to a multi-level restaurant with massive view windows overlooking the Valley business sprawl. A sleekly garbed hostess in high heeled pumps at which Meredith could only wince in imagined pain, led her to a table that sat on its own small stage surrounded by gleaming urns with waist-high metal bushes. Jay Dillington, a medium-build man, well-trimmed brownish hair with sparks of salt and pepper, well-suited but filled slightly too full, stood to greet her. His face, like his suit, was filled out a bit more than his innate boyish looks deserved. He welcomed her in not-quite-grandiose but cavalier style. Took her hand and warmly pressed it longer than called for.

Demurely she withdrew it as the waiter pulled back her chair and she sat down.

"I apologize that Ivan has had a minor interruption about tomorrow and cannot join us this evening. But I believe you'll meet him along with Todd Salem and Bob Sands in the morning for breakfast. Tonight, it's just the two of us and I'll be happy to fill you in on everything Hollywood about our new Todd Salem Studios." Dillington's words were actually good to hear. It meant Meredith had a better chance of finding the deeper more personal story behind the establishment of a movie studio to be built in a large vacant field some 10 miles away from anything associated with high technology.

The restaurant was busy yet almost eerily quiet, the service efficient and without drama, the food excellent. Meredith ordered sand dabs and gazpacho soup. Dillington, a serious sounding beef dish. Wine was paired by the restaurant. The table conversation began as any new discussants' would. Mundane, generic, backgrounding and parrying around commitment to the discussion and mission at hand: movie making. As dessert, a mellow rum chocolate mousse, was being prepared, Dillington folded his hands on the table and looked intently at Meredith.

"Do you like what you do?" he asked in a right angle subject twist.

The question took her by surprise. "Yes, yes I do," she answered with as cool a demeanor as she could muster. He looked closely into her eyes.

"Why?" She felt unnerved but constructed an immediate and concise answer.

"Tell me about your life," he probed, his voice taking on a gentle but darkly satin tone. Flustered but holding control she summarized her life: happily married, one child, satisfying career, nice home, and on and on. His eyes continued to fix on hers.

"Tell me about your life, Mr. Dillington," she quickly countered. "And do you like what you do?" She asked with an intended chuckle to ease the intensity. "I'm supposed to be the reporter here."

"Call me Jay, please, and you're going to be amazed what we are doing over there in Milpitas," he said avoiding her questions,

"You will want to be involved in it, just wait and see. We'll have a long and productive relationship, I know." He placed his index finger gently on her wrist, a move she knew to be an obvious step beyond mere dalliance. Meredith withdrew the hand, reaching for her water glass. She smiled calculating how to stop the velvet tirade she knew was more than simple flirting.

"Well, I'm looking forward to hearing more about it tomorrow," she smoothly closed off the glossy assault, then slowly rose from the table. "Please excuse me for a moment while I use the powder room. Be right back." As she stood, he followed the traditional old-school male etiquette, stood up as well.

She stared into the mirror in the women's restroom, assessing her own image as she perceived what it must be to others. Then, was almost amused that it had helped to unleash the dogs of coquettish dalliance from a "genuine Silicon Valley—legendary—mogul." That and her weighty media reputation and presence—most widely published entertainment journalist in the country—was apparently enough to catch the attention of electronic magnates turned movie producer/directors.

Normally Meredith carried a mobile phone now—a little too heavy for her small leather dinner purse—but she saw that the restaurant bathroom still had a discreetly placed wall phone for patrons. She quickly picked it up, submitted her credit card and called her husband T.K. Raymond. "In trouble already?" he teased hearing her voice.

"No but say something sexy to me, then tell me you love me and then I have to go. I'll tell you about it later." He did. She hung up and returned to the table where Jay Dillington rose to greet her. An artful cocktail—shimmering in effervescent lavender layers in a delicate flute—sat at her place. Alcohol had always been kept at a distance during work events for Meredith. Looking at the seductive offering her senses went on high alert. Stay centered, she reminded herself while pushing away stories she'd heard of women who'd been drugged and taken advantage of. But by one of the world's most infamous computer moguls? Doubtful, she thought, yet decided to be on guard.

A half hour later she'd wheedled from him quotes and some intimate thoughts about his own life, ignored some murmured less-than-credible compliments—and winks—then deemed it time to leave. She'd prudently and masterfully managed to pour most of her cocktail into the large metal urn next to her chair when Dillington was looking elsewhere. Please don't rust, she willed a wish to the receptacle.

"I've taken a penthouse suite here for some meetings and hosting visiting guests like member of the media. Would you like to join me for a nightcap and continue with any other questions you might have? I feel like we have more to discuss." His hand cupped her elbow. Either old-school chivalry, she thought, but considering he was about her own age, more like boomer control.

"Thanks," she smiled, scooting ahead of him and out of his reach as they walked through the elegant surroundings. "I'll grab a cab and head back so I can call my daughter and husband and make some notes in preparation for tomorrow. But you've been a wonderful host, a fine interview, and the dinner was superb. Compliments to the chef and your hospitality team." She quickly turned, extended her hand and shook his, then headed through the lobby and out into the entrance.

"Wait," he called. "Let me call my car for you."

"No need," she smiled over her shoulder. "It's a short distance and there's already a cab at the front." She rued her own lack of courage and confidence. Parrying with world famous electronic power brokers were not a part of her normal behavioral archive. She wasn't sure what to expect. No PR or standards person was going to mediate if something untoward happened. And exposing bad behavior in the press probably meant nothing … other than perhaps "no internet for you!" Meant for the reporter—parroting the iconic line from an early *Seinfeld* TV episode about a soup vendor who withheld soup from patrons showing bad behavior.

☆☆☆

"I can tell you more sexy stuff," Raymond told her later on the phone. "But I don't have much other advice except that I know you can take care of yourself. An electronics billionaire can't be any more trouble than a superstar."

The gurgle in Meredith's laugh was palpable. She was curled against the pillow in the hotel suite—with Raymond sprawled in the king bed in their Malibu bedroom. It was a scene that had played out many times over the years—sometimes with Meredith in the hotel room sometimes the other way around. "These guys make Hollywood sharks seem like guppies." Meredith added. "Unfettered confidence. Cocksure … " she heard Raymond snigger quietly. "We ain't seen nothin' yet! Wait until these guys take over the world. And to hear them talk—they will."

"News flash," he sputtered. "They already have."

After loudly smooching a goodnight kiss to Riley, ditto to Raymond, she hung up, then called her friend Lucy in Santa Cruz.

"How's the investigation of Hollywood in Hades?" asked the small town journalist. Meredith's chuckled response was, again, telling. "That good HUH?" Lucy responded.

"Not bad at all. Interesting but kind of defensive about not being the 'real' deal, and some side-stepping on my part around some very smooth questionable chivalry toward me."

"Dillington?"

"He have a reputation?"

"Kind of," Lucy answered. "He's kind of a horndog. Married for the third time—the last two were his secretaries. But wait, before you condemn him totally you should know that for a couple of decades, in addition to smart, educated and ambitious women migrating to the Valley for a stake in the digital future, we also had femme migrants who came looking for the newly minted—and well celebrated—genius entrepreneurs who had become the country's darling millionaires. No strategy was ignored."

"Huh. Never occurred to me," uttered Meredith.

"Well … men, you know … they are clueless until half their worth is gone with the last wife and the future wealth is already invested in the new one who's already pregnant with the insurance kid."

"Cynical," said Meredith. "And speaking of brilliant men, how's Phillip?"

"Spending his evening grading papers," Lucy laughed. "There's something far less hysterical over on this side of the hill. Can you drive over and spend a night or day with us?"

Meredith turned the invitation around and suggested Lucy come and spend Wednesday night with her in the Valley. Lucy conferred with Phillip and then heartily agreed.

"But I have a question for you for now," Meredith went on. "One of the movie studio's investors is Frogner Venture Partners. Know anything about them?"

"I've read the name here and there. One of those City firms that's made up of a lot of former tech CEOs with money."

"Some kind of weird stuff about offshore investors—maybe China," called Lucy's husband Phillip who apparently had just walked into earshot.

"Know anything more?" Meredith asked, her interest suddenly piqued. "Is Chinese investment a problem?"

"Know more?" Lucy passed along the question to her husband.

"Up for debate," he said, pouring himself a late night glass of milk. Lucy turned the phone toward him so Meredith could hear his answer. "American tech is supposedly on China's radar for serious investment but not everyone in the Valley is anxious to join up. They worry China has a bug up its ass to infiltrate the tech industry and ultimately take it over and back to the motherland. Supposedly one of China's four key American industrial targets in coming decades."

"Remember some Chinese producers like RunRun Shaw have been around in American movies for a long time," Lucy added "Although he's headquartered in Hong Kong—kind of different from Mainland China."

"For now," came the muffled comment behind her in the room.

"Huh, Yeah, *Blade Runner*," pondered Meredith, not quite knowing what to do with the information. She bid the Gillmans goodnight and retreated back into her pillows to decide if China was even her issue and if so, how. A few minutes later, she placed another call, knowing she'd probably be rousing the recipient from sleep.

"Ito. A question," she opened as the long-time colleague answered the phone in his Venice, California condominium.

A financial operative and known investment expert in the media company with which she worked, he grumbled "uh huh."

"Know anyone in the financial world who could tell us anything about Chinese investment in this movie studio they're building up here in the Silicon Valley. Supposedly a partner in an investment firm that owns a stake in it. Frogner Venture Partners out of San Francisco."

She heard the rustling as Ito pulled himself from sleep and reached for his glasses, a pen and paper.

"Tell me again," he said in a more gathered voice. "And I'll call you tomorrow. Will you have your mobile with you?"

"You bet," she affirmed, repeated her questions for him, then snapped off the light and turned toward sleep, herself.

☆ ☆ ☆

Tuesday began with the suite phone ringing as Meredith adjusted her 'I ♥ L.A.' t-shirt and well-tailored cargo pants ready for climbing around the raw fields in Milpitas later in the day. According to her host Rob Hatman, no one would be dressing for magazine covers. She snatched up the receiver, aware of the breakfast meeting time looming.

"Are you here for the unveiling?" came the warm but gravelly voice of her old friend, former boss, Fred Barton. For the past ten years Fred had been the editor of one of the entertainment industries' most prestigious weekly trade publications. They'd remained close collaborative colleagues since working together at an L.A. TV network two decades earlier.

"Here, yes. For the unveiling, yes. Like a Felliniesque scene, Fred."

"Somehow I guessed it would be and flew up late last night in time for the falderal."

"Hey—these folks are deadly serious. Be careful of how frivolous you make it sound."

"Serious my ass!"

"Language, Fred."

"All right. Anything I should know about before the noon press conference and groundbreaking?"

"Oh, they'll tell you everything they want you to know. Big, fat glossy press kit, hot shot PR people to usher us all around tomorrow. You'd think this was the premiere of a long lost version of *Gone With the Wind*."

"What are you doing before the noon flack fest?"

"Breakfast first with the big shots. Then back to the room, I guess, for a couple of hours of work. I'm at Rickeys. If you're close by, come on by and let's compare press kits."

"Call me when you get in from breakfast. I'll ride with you to the presser."

✩ ✩ ✩

"The technology of movie making hasn't been my most top-of-mind subject matter," Meredith confessed to her hosts—two tech giants, two public relations representatives and one Hollywood superstar. She found the conversation over corned beef hash and other morning delectables repetitive—of each other and their motives for movie studio creation. And uninformative. They'd been press-prepared very well.

"My one question remains the same for all," she explained, preparing for a cordial wrap up of the session. "Why a movie studio here? A huge investment with a gargantuan road ahead to produce good films, find writers, directors, actors who aren't split in half between your studio and those already established in more entertainment centers—actually around the world?"

"Because, as you of all people certainly know," said the obvious godfather of the group Ivan Milsap, "Hollywood is everywhere now. It's not just a city where Sunset and Vine Streets cross. It's a worldwide industry seeping into all parts of the world. But notice that every successful, future-focused studio is dependent on new technologies, ways of creating imagery, filling a screen, thrilling the viewers—from the earliest days of movies, production technologies like cameras, lenses, sound. And those technologies are, by and large, coming from these factories and labs sprinkled throughout Northern California. Companies with the brain trust and dedication to reach beyond the trite image we have of 'Hollywood.'" He took a drink of coffee, then continued, "And 'Silicon Valley' is a little like the idea of 'Hollywood'—it's not just confined to the length of this peninsula. It's morphed into Austin, Texas, Boston, Colorado, and many, many other centers not even in the U.S. It's a concept. An idea and a commitment." He shrugged. Meredith sat back realizing she was hearing the "word" from someone who had the knowledge and the history to say it. She was humbled.

"If you think of the most obvious examples," Ivan went on, "George Lucas and Industrial Light and Magic—*Star Wars*—*Indiana Jones*. Pixar—blooming out of electronics labs and shepherded by Apple's Steve Jobs. Nolan Bushnell whose people developed the visual effects and mechanisms of Pong and so many games, Chuck E. Cheese has a movie in prep. Bet you didn't know about that. Those are the famous names but there're so many others. Ideas if not born and bred around here, then certainly inspired and trained … " Ivan took a breath.

Meredith shook her head and politely waved Ivan off before he continued. "I'm truly a little abashed," she said. "I haven't thought of the tech side of 'seen-ay-mah' … " she exaggerated "cinema," to call attention to high-culture movie aficionados. "I hope Rob can pass along a little more history."

"Thank you," said Ivan, "for listening and for asking."

☆☆☆

"Meredith Ogden humbled," mused Fred Barton, reclining on a sofa in the hotel lobby an hour later. "Something to behold!" Meredith glared at him and extended her middle finger.

"I see a lot more about movie tech at my weekly industry rag than you do in your celebrity gig," he went on, "but kind of surprised these guys taking it from science lab to a commercial movie studio. I guess in their minds the connection to a studio of their own makes sense. Although it wasn't an original thought." He started then paused. "I do know something about this and hadn't thought of it in years."

He sat forward and scratched his ear. "I think this may have been the original brainchild of Sal Luck." Meredith looked at him, confused.

"Sal Luck—comic book, comic studio stuff. *Wonderstuff* comics, animated films. Sal was the original founder/cartoonist and writer of *Nutsy*. The wacky humor magazine from the 1950s. I talked to him a few years ago before he passed away and he was still lamenting that his efforts at convincing the animation and tech 'assholes' hadn't advanced plans they'd already put into motion about a Silicon Valley movie studio."

"Forward thinker."

"Too bad he wasn't such a great businessman. So much of his work that's now really iconic was never patented, copyrighted, and his estate—whatever it looks like—doesn't get much benefit from his creativity and brilliance."

Meredith tilted her coffee cup back and forth, heavy

concentration in her eyes. "Fred, did you interview him all those years ago about the idea of a tech movie studio?"

"Yeah. I remember talking with him in depth about it at Pink's Hot Dog Stand in L.A. It was his favorite place to eat!

"He was fired up because the Silicon Valley boys had come to some kind of agreement that was being drafted. But it wasn't a long or very detailed story as I remember. Very little detail—confidential, he said. And I never remember hearing anything more about it. Certainly won't be visible in the festivities today."

"Can you find your interview in the pub's archives? Could I get a copy? Might be an interesting aside for the story I'll write."

"Sure, probably to both. I'll call and get someone at the office on it today. When are you filing your story?" asked Fred. "Mine goes out tonight for tomorrow—but just a newsy piece, no big deal. I'll do a more in depth follow-up sometime later."

Meredith glanced at her notes. "This afternoon just a news story about the groundbreaking for tomorrow's wire. Next week the more in-depth piece—but not any competition to you since our readers are very different. I'll eventually do a feature on superstar Todd with his name on this studio as the hook. No rush on him," Meredith added wryly.

☆☆☆

Mid-day after the groundbreaking ceremony with its phalanx of photographers and local and international media, civic dignitaries and studio principals, an elaborate picnic lunch was served. In a perfect blue-skied, not yet crisp, October, gazebo-style canopies had been placed along the grounds of the former squash fields, buffet tables laden with sandwiches, salads and savory baked goods beckoned to the group. Jeans-clad wait staff served cold beer and wine and soft drinks.

Meredith met up with a news videographer who would film a location shot with her interviewing actor Todd Salem and Ivan

Milsap. The footage would be sent to her colleague/producer Cassie O'Connell in L.A. and used with Meredith's usual appearance that week on a TV morning show.

As the filming wrapped and cameras were being stowed, Meredith and Milsap unclipped their microphones, and she turned to the older man, posing an intentionally casual question. "Was that comic guy—*Wonderstuff* creator—Sal Luck ever part of your team? I seem to recall him being involved years ago in some sort of plans to set up movie making right here in the Valley."

Milsap peered at her and grinned. "You have a good memory or good resources." He pulled off his jacket and sat down on a bench wearily. "I'm an old man and don't usually spend anywhere near this much energy in a day."

"It's a big day for you, Ivan," Meredith agreed, sitting down on the bench next to him, emitting a sigh of her own. He reached into his pants pocket and extracted a somewhat beat-up cigar.

"Mind?" he asked. She shook her head. He took a match book from his shirt pocket and lit up.

"But Sal Luck?" she persisted.

Always the gentleman, Ivan leaned back, tilted his head toward the sky and wrinkled his brow. "Long time ago," he sighed, puffing from the cigar. "And not a lot of detail in my memory. I do recall lots of discussion around setting up this type of a deal with a studio kind of based on Sal's characters and comics. He was just starting to produce movies—or his people were—then. And Sal himself was dedicated to the future of technology. Remember he started out as an animator and went from there to special effects and on and on."

"But no actual studio development took place?" Meredith pressed. Ivan shook his basketball-shaped bald head. "It was in the hands of Bill Pokka. He was one of the early integrated circuits guys—specialized stuff—and fantasized he'd supply the movie industry with unique ICs for unique productions—pie-in-the-sky. Before that happened, he had some 'trouble' with taxes, let's say, his company was sold to … well, and then to and then to … . Bob Sands now owns what remains of Bill's old firm. The plans disappeared as fast as Bill did. I've heard nothing since about the studio. Bill, maybe something about Belize or Costa Rica … " The electronics mogul scratched his head and smiled at Meredith. "And we are here today. Are you getting a good story?"

Meredith burst out in a loud guffaw. "How can I not?" she gulped. "It's not often a destination wedding between Hollywood and Silicon Vallely takes place—and I get to be on the front lines. With the founding fathers. Ivan, I'm fascinated and honored—and also full of material and stories. You've all been amazing. I do have one question, however." Milsap nodded.

"I saw hardly any women here except for assistants and the videographer my TV studio hired. Not even among all the press liaisons. That seems unusual to me."

Ivan shrugged and flayed his hands in resignation, the smoldering cigar hanging from his fingers. "Each of the principals here—me, Sands, Dillington, even the VC folks and the movie star—contributed their own PR person. I hired Rob because he has the best knowledge of anyone in the Valley about the history. And he's well connected—as you know, you being an old friend of his. Dillington's guy has been with the company as long as Jay has, and Sands' guy was his college roommate. Apparently not a very good engineer but is pretty good as a PR flack."

"It's interesting to me, is all," murmured Meredith, a little perplexed by the reality, thinking, it really is an old boys' club—even now.

"And," Ivan added, standing up. "We're tired. How about you?" She chuckled and agreed. They shook hands, bid a farewell with a promise to be in touch whenever necessary and headed toward their own destinations.

★★★

"A fax came for you Ms. Ogden," the desk clerk at the hotel called to Meredith as she made her way through the lobby area to the outside walkways leading to her garden room. She took the two pages handed to her and glanced through them as she went to the suite. Puzzled, she dumped her handbag and briefcase onto the sofa and sat down to study the fax more closely. It had come from Ito with background on her question about Chinese investors in Frogner Venture Capital.

"I don't quite understand it, Ito. Maybe I'm just ignorant about financial issues and investment," she launched into a phone discussion with her colleague who had the financial grounding. "It seems like there's a Chinese partner in the VC firm—how big a partner interest, whether there's any involvement in the movie studio and if so how big an involvement … and is it really anything of importance? All that kind of thing."

"I only got this far," Ito explained. "But I'll try to dig deeper. He disconnected."

She settled into the suite, looked around and stripped off her dusty, gritty clothes that had seen her through several hours in Milpitas' former squash and corn fields, then made her way into the shower. She smiled as she soaped her hair and let the warm water course across her body and carry away the day, remembering when hotel showers signaled time to call Raymond—now her husband but for years simply the man she lived with and held both her heart and her body! She blushed even in her solitude and felt the pull of heat whenever she thought of Raymond and … well … all of him. She thought of the many, many nights one or the other of them were harbored in one or another hotel or motel room on an assignment away from home—cheap roadside inns to high-ticket resorts—and settled in on the phone making small talk—and more. With a five-year-old daughter now, showers, bedtime and most everything else were different today.

At four o'clock she sat down to compose her first article—seven hundred and fifty words that told the basic news about the tech giants, a superstar and a VC company developing a movie studio in the Silicon Valley. An hour later she called home, talked with Riley about her day in kindergarten, assuring her she'd be back in time for the youngster's Halloween play—sending kisses to both Riley and yes, Paco the cat, who divided his own feline time between the top of the kitchen refrigerator and Riley's every move.

And then came the knock announcing pal Lucy's arrival from Santa Cruz. Meredith rushed to the door and flung it open to embrace her long-time friend. Naturally curly brown hair askew, a figure as athletic and supple as Meredith's, Lucy lugged in her shoulder bag containing her overnight necessities and looked around. "Nice digs. Glad the village appreciates your presence and importance!" Meredith laughed and offered a glass of wine from the mini fridge.

Later, over shrimp and steak dishes at nearby Valley dining mainstay, Dinah's Shack, Meredith and Lucy had meandered through their life since college days, caught up with the gossip on old friends, and landed on today's reality. "But I don't get why you closed up shop in the Valley," Meredith puzzled to Lucy. "You had a great reputation, really fast upward mobility as far as those of us who weren't among the anointed, and your own advertising agency. What?"

Lucy plied a combination of grin and grimace in the effervescence of the margarita she was drinking. "I just wasn't built for the predatory nature of the village inhabitants here. And it is a village, make no mistake." Meredith tilted her head with question.

"Women didn't seem to have any role but helper in the earliest days. I got here about 1975 with a math degree, a master's degree in marketing and an unrealistic expectation. Foolish me. At first, I was wooed and recruited by the handful of brand new ad agencies and existing, emerging companies because of—I thought—my knowledge and potential abilities as a professional. Then I realized that the path was recruit first, seduce next, promise to promote and share and never deliver. Meanwhile, all us femme-potentials traipsed around making the male managers, principals, autocrats look good and gain cache while keeping their egos and libidos well exercised. One place I worked, there was kind of a "friend club" made up of single secretaries and underlings with on-going ties to the management troop. One or another of them. These ladies met, dined together, shared stories and supported the status quo. Most of their boyfriends were married to someone else."

Meredith shook her head. "I've heard of groups like that—but they're not exclusive to high tech."

"No, but it is prevalent—and apparently acceptable."

"Still today?" asked Meredith.

Lucy nodded and took a drink of her margarita. "Not as noticeable as it was. A bunch of us professionals banded together and started an association just for women in the communication and marketing fields. There are nearly 500 members now and that has helped nudge and force some upward movement for women—and some awareness that they are not just arm pieces who can type and work with spread sheets—or as one put it: spread-ed sheets." She chuckled at her own joke.

"But you had your own business. And were married, yourself. Phillip was involved in the software industry, wasn't he?"

"Yeah, yeah and yeah. But the women became as cutthroat as their male role models. The professional women—qualified or, as the management expert Herzberg called them—'counterfeit professionals', were wanna-be vice presidents—of something—and were willing to do whatever it took to snag that. Colleague-leap-frogging and back-stabbing was a way of life, so you needed a suit of armor to fend off the professional assaults. And a really strong sense of righteousness. A good mentor helped but since most were male with all the proclivities of the insecure geek, the association most often gave you a free pass to the monthly 'let's sleep with the boss' gang." Lucy smirked, took a drink of her cocktail, and stared at the ceiling for a moment.

"I side-stepped the boss's affections," she continued thoughtfully, "and then his reprisals and additional assaults by opening my own agency, especially after one of my supposedly collegial managers decided she wanted her name on the agency door, so set out to destroy my reputation and standing. Turned out, even walking a straight and narrow sex life as I tried to do, my predator didn't particularly identify with the 'hetero-persuasion' and any social outings I took were duly documented and called into question as 'possible conflicts of interest.' When Phillip and I married, we went to Boston where he's from. Never announced it locally for weeks, and so it was kind of fun retribution to finally mention it to my agency colleagues, boss and power stalker who was still spreading rumors of my indiscretions. When I opened my own business, I managed another stupid misstep by inviting in as a junior partner one of my former female colleagues who seemed on the same path as me. But alas, her eyes were also on whatever prize was available—my business."

The swarthy brunette shook her head in disgust. "She managed to snatch away the firm when I took a 45-day forced leave of absence to be with my mother who was slipping way in hospice in Illinois."

"Didn't you sue the partner or … fire her … or, I don't know—something to take back your firm?"

"No, I sold out at fire sale prices, paid off my own start-up costs and left. Phillip was on board with the move away from it all. What happened to me sickened him enough to actually lead the charge. He's a much happier guy teaching finance and economics than trying to cover the mistakes and overreaches of spoiled children with high IQs. I was then—and am now—done with the Valley and all it portends."

"Do you miss the thrill of the new ideas, new developments … what seems like infinite exploration? The highs of new discoveries, adrenalin. All the stuff of technology birthing?"

"No. And I hear enough, being only an hour away, to do some occasional stringing for major pubs like the *LA Times* and others—and I get my fill of the thrill of new discovery … " Lucy drained the last of her drink.

"Ooh—Mata Hari," snickered Meredith. "Not just cynical.

Just a tad vengeful?"

"Not at all," grinned Lucy. "Entitled."

☆☆☆

In the hotel suite, a sofa bed was made up for Lucy when the duo returned. The two women put in a call to her husband Phillip with questions they both developed over their dinner chatter. Mostly about the presence of Chinese money in the electronics industry—even if only in the form of a movie studio. He reminded them that the Japanese were already usurping much of U.S. electronics manufacturing and that globalization of this rapidly and vastly growing market sector was broadening.

"It's only logical the Chinese are at the gate," said Lucy's economist husband.

"How does the American electronics industry feel about that." Meredith asked.

She could almost feel Phillip shrugging and yet wincing at the other end of the line. "Well … " He hesitated. "Money's money. Cheap labor counts a lot, and, and … and … international trade seems to morph in strange ways in all manufacturing sectors. My own concern is that not today but in the future all these folks starting to trade microchips and components with lots of other countries will eventually snap upright and wonder what happened to our American economic root system." He said no more.

Meredith waved her hands. "Above my pay grade and beyond my need. Enough background. I'm going to bed." She blew a kiss to Lucy still holding on to the receiver connected to Phillip.

Behind the closed door of the bedroom, Meredith initiated her own call home—completing it with murmurs and chuckles with Raymond. "My turn to ask you," he said, "what are you wearing?"

"Nothing. Dream about that, hot stuff." She brayed a kiss and hung up.

Drifting off to sleep, Meredith was awakened by a persistent knocking on the suite door. She unfurled herself from the covers, slid out of bed, moving toward the sound. Pushing open the bedroom door, she saw Lucy sitting up in the sofa bed, shaking her head, confused. The knocking continued. Looking carefully through the entry's small peep hole, she called, "Who is it?" already recognizing the face of Jay Dillington, her lothario dinner interview from the night before.

"It's Jay!" he yelled, "and I have great news for you."

Looking at Lucy, she put a "shhh" finger to her lips. "What is it, Mr. Dillington?" she asked loudly, leaving the door closed and locked.

"Hey, journalist lady. 'Member I told you about the evening get togethers in the penthouse? Well, we're having a big one tonight and you might pick up some good gossip. Come on up. I promise you a good time. I personally guarantee it." His words were slightly slurred.

"No thanks," Meredith called out "Have a good night." She closed off the conversation and continued to shush Lucy whose eyes had grown wide above a wry smirk.

"Horndog," she whispered. Meredith put a hand over her own mouth to stifle a chuckle. Dillington launched one more set of knocks, seemed to stand in front of the door for a few more seconds then lumbered down the walkway, grumbling something incoherent.

Both women in the room held their breath and stayed at attention until it seemed the corridor outside was empty of Dillington. "This happen often to you?" Lucy chuckled.

"Not often but enough. Too much tonight," Meredith growled. "Go back to sleep—I need some more," she added as she padded back into the bedroom and tumbled into the covers, reaching for the light to bring back the darkness.

★★☆

"Oh, oh, here he comes," murmured Lucy to Meredith as the two were having breakfast in the hotel dining room. A slightly travel-worn Jay Dillington was making his way toward them. His full figure was wrapped in warm-up togs—fashionable but only a slight boost for his grayish skin belying a long night of non-athletic recreation.

Meredith took a deep breath and went on the offensive. "Jay—good to see you're on deck and on point this morning." The roundish tech mogul made his way toward the duo, his hand extended in greeting to Lucy. "Jay," he said, reaching to shake hers. Thank God, Meredith thought to herself, this table only seats two.

"You look like you're off for racquetball or running," she spoke up to Dillington, hoping to close off the conversation. "We won't keep you."

He hesitated, standing firmly. "Do you have all the information you need, Meredith?" he persisted. "Any last-minute questions?"

At that moment, Meredith saw an opening for a tough question that had lurked in her mind, but had crouched there reluctantly for fear of being considered "stupid." "I do have a question, Jay. How do you all feel about having a Chinese investor involved in your movie studio, especially one with a major position, in light of the currently industry-wide—and national trade—concern about China targeting U.S. electronics and manufacturing?"

Dillington eyes semi-fluttered in surprise. He was grasping for an appropriate and safe response but had not been prepared for the subject much less a direct question. "I … I'm not exactly up on the ownership percentages," he stumbled. "But I'd be more than happy to get back to you on it." The man was already subtly and physically backing away. Practically tap dancing, Meredith mused.

She grabbed her purse, reached in, and pulled out a business card and a pen. Circling the fax number on the card, she handed it to him, instructing, "If you could get back to me by tomorrow, I'd appreciate it. I'll be writing my article when I get home this afternoon and tomorrow for release early next week." She smiled congenially. Dillington looked at her with a confidently-posed, "you bet," and bid them good morning, practically loping through the restaurant and out the door.

"Nicely played," snuffed Lucy. "Think he'll get back to you?"

"If he doesn't, I'll still get an answer. I'm calling Rob Hatman next and asking him to get someone's response to the question— now that it's out there." The two rose from their table, leaving money with the breakfast bill, and headed for a quick tour of Stanford and then delivering Meredith to the San Jose Airport and the trip home.

At the terminal curb, cars jogged around Lucy's station wagon and passengers—coming and going—surged along the sidewalk as she hugged her friend. "Short visit but quite a ride," said Lucy. "And only one night and a morning!"

Meredith laughed hard, promised longer visits and invited Lucy and Phillip to join her for a long week-end in Malibu. Then turned briskly and walked into the terminal toward her flight home.

☆☆☆

"You sure this is a good idea?" Gloria Masner, Los Angeles legal maven, stylish trophy wife, and best friend of Meredith Ogden, posed the question to her journalist pal. "You're chasing ghost turds of a story. You don't seem to have any real info that's not years old and may not be even relevant."

Driving up the 101 freeway heading toward I-5 and Simi Valley, Meredith scowled. "I just feel like there's more to the story of Sal Luck and the tech movie studio. And if his name should be included—or even if his estate should be benefiting from it, it's not only a good story—a worthwhile afternoon drive through the San Fernando Valley." The relatively newly developed residential destination of Simi Valley boasted an earthen bowl created by golden brown humpback hills filled with low-story, stucco-looking California contemporary living. Ranch houses, fast food shopping strips, commuters from Los Angeles and other nearby centers where the real estate was more costly than in Simi.

Meredith had invited her lawyer-friend Gloria along on a visit to descendants of comic fantasy icon Sal Luck—whoever might constitute "the family" and however they related to the late brilliant innovator. Meredith's assistant Sonia had ferreted out the remaining Luck heirs and survivors—not many—and found a relatively close location. Meredith had set up an afternoon visit. They knew she was a journalist revisiting the work of their father/grandfather. She suspected some discussion might ensue about contracts, rights and other legal entanglements and Gloria would have insight Meredith herself did not.

Gloria handled the Thomas Brothers map, guiding Meredith who navigated through the well-kept streets. Pulling up in front of one of the typical one-story, white-washed structures, surrounded by a well-kept lawn and series of hedges and flower beds, both women took a look at the map page to confirm the address. "I would have expected something larger or more opulent," snicked Gloria. "A world-celebrated comic hero."

"Well, Ivan told me Sal was a bad businessman and lost out on a lot of the residuals and income from his own work," Meredith recounted. The women glanced at one another, often a trigger for the start point of a new project. They left the car to approach the house. A small porch led to the brightly painted yellow front door. Meredith pushed he bell and heard a short mellifluous jingle before the door was opened by a pleasant older woman, broad smile and silver hair. A small child hugged her leg. She looked up at the visitors with a combination of suspicion and curiosity. "Meredith Ogden?" she asked.

"Hi. Thanks for seeing us," Meredith began. "I'm only here to talk for a few minutes about your father, Sal Luck." The hostess nodded, still on semi-alert.

Elizabeth Luck Garten welcomed them somewhat hesitantly into the house. "He's been dead for twenty years, and there's not much new to say any more."

Meredith persisted. "I just want to fill in the blanks on a story about movies and technology I'm working on, and Sal was one of the originators—creative minds—involved in those early days. I promise I only have a question or two. I hope it's not inconvenient." She handed Elizabeth her press credentials and a business card. Elizabeth studied Meredith and Gloria and apparently decided they didn't look like burglars or serial killers and invited them into the house. The child, a small boy of three or four years of age scurried away down a hall.

"Salvatore is my grandson and he's shy. We sometimes get curiosity addicts," said Elizabeth. "How they find us I don't know but most are rude. He's learned to hide from them."

"I'm so sorry. I can only imagine." She launched into the purpose of her visit and the story she was working on about the new tech-sponsored movie studio and how Sal Luck's name had emerged in the course of a conversation with one of the tech founders. Elizabeth chortled and shook her head of tousled silver hair. "My father's been gone for two decades, and that studio was a big deal ten years before that. But, like a lot of his dreams of fame and fortune, it went nowhere. They had meetings, signed contracts, talked with bankers and then ... and then ... well tech became bigger than the movie making. I guess the whole project went on the back burner."

"Did Sal try to resurrect it? He was so innovative I'm so surprised it never happened."

Elizabeth shook her head again. "He had so many other things happening and constant legal issues which he stumbled over but in the long run chose to just shake it off."

"What other legal issues?"

"Don't get me started. It's not my battle and I'm not the one who knows any of the legalities or even the realities. Lots of articles written about it."

"And then?" Meredith added, "He left a legacy that practically launched an entire form of humor, entertainment, movie making."

"Yeah," winced Elizabeth. "Sal was like a creative Viking—slashing through ideas and development—books, comic books, cartoons, movies—and the infamous movie studio. But not much about establishing rights or patents or even residuals." The woman pulled herself back from the discourse. "Look around. You see anything of the brilliance, the innovation of … except for the posters and pictures around the house?"

"What happened?" Gloria spoke up. "He must have had advisors, lawyers, agents … " Elizabeth shook her head.

"Some," she said. "But mostly hangers-on, and not enough. All focused on their own greed. And dad never really thought about his own future—only about the future of his characters or his stories or work. Some rights he sold cheaply to finance development of newer creative endeavors. Books, cartoon series, even the concepts and characters. Didn't even patent the work to protect it." She glanced at her own folded hands in her lap. It was a story she'd told before and was tired of, Meredith could see.

"We didn't lose out totally," she bounced in. "My daughter got the best nursing degree there was. My son in law is getting a nighttime law degree and little Salvatore will have whatever education he wants. We put what came from dad's world into something we believed had legs—education. But for the rest of it … " she gestured around her own head, "we're fine."

"The movie studio?" asked the journalists. Elizabeth shook her head. "Back burner went into the trash, I guess. Up in smoke along with other rubble. Mom always felt it was pie-in-the-sky, anyhow."

"Sal was your father. Your mother?" Gloria chimed in.

"She moved to a small retirement center in Ventura. Passed away about five years ago. She was happy there and glad to be away from what she called 'the dreaded L.A.' No one felt or saw the demise of the glittering halo around dad like she did—as one legacy after another disappeared into someone else's pocket after pocket.

Salvatore … ” she nodded her head toward the hallway and sounds of a TV, “is my grandson. His mother's a nurse. No one even knows she's the granddaughter of the great Sal Luck. Little Sal's father is a fireman—soon to be lawyer. It's a robust household Ms. Ogden. But hardly the kind of heritage you'd expect from the public persona you know about.”

“Robust households are worth more than most Hollywood bank accounts,” murmured Meredith. The room was silent for a while.

“Do you have any idea if there's a copy of the original movie agreement anywhere?” Gloria spoke up carefully without affect, working to keep the tone level with the discussion. Without drama or expectation. Elizabeth shook her head.

“Any of my father's papers are in a couple of boxes in the basement or with his former law firm in Century City. You're welcome to look through them. Not sure what you'd find but stacks of disappointments and what-if's.”

“Would you be willing to give me permission to do that?” asked Gloria. “I promise to respect your privacy, but we're working on a story about the infamous Silicon Valley studio, and it would be helpful to know a little more of the original idea.”

“Okay, I guess. Maybe there's even something in it that's relevant now,” Elizabeth agreed. “We can go look today if you'd like and have the time. It shouldn't take long.” Gloria and Meredith both nodded a carefully orchestrated agreement. “Let me know if you find a residual or two.” They all laughed politely.

Two hours later, a file with yellowing pages and a permission note in hand from Elizabeth, Meredith and Gloria were back on the freeway.

“What just happened?” murmured Gloria.

“We just scored a rare win. I think. We won't know until we study the documents thoroughly, but … ”

“But,” echoed Gloria. “When's your story due?”

“I ran the basic news story last week. I'm running the happy studio-named-after-him Todd Salem's story about his connection to the project this week. The deep-dive examination will go as quickly as I have the last of the information that fits."

Gloria let out an exaggerated sigh. "Be careful with this one. It's not about someone trying to silence you with a gun or knife, Merri. It's about the worst kind of predators—lawyers."

☆☆☆

"Ito, Ito," Meredith grumbled to herself. "I was hoping you'd say something about Chinese involvement in high technology different from what everyone else is saying … caution!"

"There's not much else to say right now, Meredith," chortled the slight Japanese man, long-time colleague of the journalist. "My people—Japan—only started importing electronic parts back about a decade and a half ago, and then the American manufacturers were not very welcoming. Japan now owns about 35% of the world's Silicon chip market. So—just look ahead a couple of decades and guess how the Chinese will fare. That's the debate. No one doubts they'll be a huge player. Not everyone's sure they want it and this is one more toe in the American market."

"But a movie studio, Ito?"

The ever-youthful countenance scowled and said, "Really, Meredith? It's already happening—aside from the Silicon Valley. Tons of foreign investment. Lots of outside interests. You know the story about how the producers of *The Godfather* movie negotiated with organized crime?" They both groaned with acknowledgment.

Her own official response from the studio management came from Rob Hatman. It said, they are pleased to have the VC company with its strength and knowledge of technology and film making and have contractual assurances that off-shore intrusion will not occur. All members of the VC partnership have been enthusiastic, effective and productive … . Yada yada yada … , she thought to herself.

Later, Meredith put in a call to her managing director at

News—New York, Russ Talbot, to talk about Chinese investment.

"Let it go, Meredith," he told her. "I'll pass on the notes to our international desk, but don't put yourself in the crosshairs just because it sounds like a sexy odor to sniff out. You'd need a lot more time and expertise in areas that aren't easily accessed. Mention Chinese investment in your article but move on." In the quiet of her office, Meredith checked "Chinese connection" off her list of research topics.

She girded herself for the next and last item on the list—Sal Luck. She hesitantly picked up the phone receiver pursing her lips and she punched in the number she read from the card Ivan Milsap had given her. She'd already attempted to speak with the other tech partners—Dillington and Sands. Both had brushed her off generally saying, "I don't know anything about Sal Luck and he's never been part of our discussions or strategy." Which she already knew was not true.

Her call was put through immediately to Milsap. Ivan's cultured voice greeted her without hesitation. "Meredith Ogden. I was just thinking about you and realizing I should have called you to see if you had all the information and help from us you need for whatever you're writing about our project." She thanked him and told him she had a couple of further questions about Sal Luck. Ivan chuckled.

"I never think of that man without a smile on my face. Everything he did was brilliance and so much humor. A jokester."

"I hope taking him seriously wasn't part of the joke," Meredith mused, keeping the conversation light. Ivan's confusion at the other end of the line was palpable in the silence.

"I'd kind of like to talk with you a bit more about what Sal's actual involvement was, Ivan. You mentioned he was one of the original team to take this movie studio forward, but it got pushed to—I think you said, 'the back burner'—and never came forward again."

"That's right," Ivan confirmed. "Two years ago, we resur-rected the project. The same group of people were involved, joined by several more. Initially, the group was comprised of young just-made millionaires. And the first thing they thought about after buying the houses in Martha's Vineyard and Maui, was jumping into the movie industry."

"Like everyone, they just wanted to direct movies," Meredith added in jest.

"I suppose," Ivan answered with a chuckle. "But the recent group expanded the agreement with addendums as well as a couple more partners. Sal's name doesn't appear anywhere. You can find out more if you talk with the attorney representing us … " He named a familiar barrister in the San Francisco area. Meredith knew of the guy and also preferred to avoid any more chatter than necessary. "He has the original agreement and how it was amended," Ivan added.

"Did anyone contact Sal's family or heirs?"

"I only recall it was discussed but the way the thing was structured, everything was a grey area and the last I heard we were simply moving forward with the group now involved."

"I have the original agreement, Ivan." Meredith explained. "I talked with Sal's daughter and family right here in Southern California. They have the same recollection you do. The back burner just burned up and nothing was left from the ashes." Silence ensued as Ivan seemed to ponder the comment.

"And," Meredith continued, "it seems like the property was purchased back in the original days—as a separate entity from the movie studio developers—and leased back to the studio developers. It looks like Sal Luck was one of the investor/owners of that property. The one in Milpitas. Did someone buy him out? Or has he or any of his heirs been privy to any of the lease rents coming from the property?"

Silence again until Ivan spoke up hesitantly and quietly. "I'm not sure, Meredith. In all truth, I've not been involved in any of the latter day dealing until now. And I'm now only participating actively because I was asked to do so—supposedly because of my stature in the Valley—my name. That doesn't excuse me though, from being a part of any inequities. That's just my error in judgment. Bill Pokka handled most of the business and arrangements around this property and movie studio. He left years ago and, as I think I told you, his assets, company—the whole cream puff—became Bearbite, Bob Sands' domain. May I look into this?"

"I'd appreciate it, Ivan, but I do have to go to press day after tomorrow. I can't put off the whole studio story any longer or it loses its immediacy—its relevance."

"I can call you back as quickly as possible. I will find out about this. I can't really think that someone as vital and visible as Sal Luck would be disregarded, just cut out. Discarded."

"Thank you, Ivan. But as overdramatic as it sounds—be careful."

"Yuh," he snuffed. "I'll call you in the morning."

As Meredith hung up the phone, her cynicism rose up. Like that'll happen, she thought.

The rest of the day passed. Evening was filled with the chatter and clatter of Riley's kindergarten day, lively exchanges with the dinner guest—Raymond's half-brother Tad Oakley who left to drive home to Irvine, California, about ninety minutes south. The Silicon Valley movie studio notes sat on Meredith desk, taking their own evening off.

☆☆☆

Savoring the steam from a fresh cup of coffee the next morning, Meredith contemplated the workday ahead. Tuesday. No TV appearance, not Sonia's day in the office, Riley off to school, Raymond to detecting. Lupe, the housekeeper, cleaning the kitchen soon to be managing the laundry. Meredith sat down and began to dig into her notes and partial drafts of the movie studio article. In the background the *Morning Coffee* TV show droned on, the program she normally appeared on one day a week and was produced by her long-time friend and colleague Cassie O'Connell.

Another mini-TV monitor had a silenced *Today Show* running. One short news brief along with a few minutes of commentary by Jay Dillington had appeared in the various media the week before—the evening after the Milpitas groundbreaking. Meredith's story would eclipse all other mentions with its depth and weight.

By eleven, no word had come from Ivan. Meredith karmically shrugged and began to structure the story when the phone rang with Ivan's voice in greeting. "Where can we meet," came his controlled but obviously hypered voice. "I have some documents but I need to see you and I'm in Ventura."

Head reeling to understand Ivan's current location and situation, Meredith stammered. "What are you doing in Ventura, Ivan and what documents. Are you okay?"

"Yes," Ivan seemed to gasp. "I called the attorney yesterday and asked about a copy of the sales agreement for Milpitas. He didn't return my call. I guess I just wasn't thinking straight and told his secretary what I needed. She said he was out for the day. So, I went into the Fairweather files at our headquarters here. Never been there before but the librarian and I dug deep and found a lot of information I really don't want to know." His voice had accelerated and amplified with stress.

"That was yesterday and when I was about to go home, Willa, my house manager, called me to say that two people from the venture capital firm had stopped by the house to see me. She said they didn't seem like legit barristers' reps, were vague about who they worked for. Rude and demanding. Willa knows how to interrogate, believe me. She's run my household since my wife Laura passed, five years ago. They told her they would be back last night when I was home. I remember you telling me to 'be careful.' I told Willa to pack an overnight bag for me and meet me at her sister's house in Saratoga. She's staying there right now and I'm on my way to see you about this stuff I have in my briefcase. Where's your office?"

Meredith started to relay her home office address when she

caught herself. "Ivan, don't come here. If, in fact, these guys are any kind of threat—I'm assuming because of the questions about Sal Luck's involvement or legal rights or—I'd be the first place anyone would look or contact. Where are you in Ventura?" Ivan told her he was parked at a gas station.

"Stay there and I'll call you right back. Give me your mobile phone number." He did. She dropped her head into her hands to think about where Ivan could hole up safely and meet her. Then it came to her. Alan Jaymar, her old friend and former agent. He and his partner lived in a delightful retirement community in Calabasas, only about forty-five minutes from Ventura. More importantly, reasoned Meredith, Alan was one of the few people she knew would be comfortable and on a par with Ivan's standing in the computer world. Alan had mentored and managed more celebrities and egos than anyone else Meredith knew. And the two men were of the same generation. She put in the call to Alan and was met with instant agreement. "We don't see many outsiders these days," mused Alan. "Send him on."

She did. Soon Ivan was on his way to Calabasas.

☆☆☆

At two that afternoon, Meredith, herself, arrived at Alan's condominium. He welcomed her heartily and she knew that the guest had found a hospitable safehouse and the host was intrigued by his guest. She hated to break up the pleasant talk fest, but knew she had to make haste on new information in order to meet her weekly deadline. Most of the story had been told with room for embellishment as she found out new data.

She did.

"Order pizza," she told Raymond from her car phone. "I have to finish this story tonight and I hope no one gets murdered for this information. It's public record if you know where to find it, but I guess the partners didn't want it revealed. Or, at least one of them didn't. I can only guess why."

"Money," Raymond said flatly.

"Not wanting to share. But the VC firm took the lead on the legal stuff for all this studio development and I'm not sure the older partners were even aware that Sal was—first, ever really involved it was so long ago and it was casual a thing—and second, he was very subtly extracted for all discussions, documents. Apparently under the hand of a very early player, Bill Pokka. I wouldn't have known of it at all if Fred hadn't remembered an old interview with Sal. Neither would Ivan, it seems."

"Need I say, be careful," murmured Raymond.

"No—you need not," sighed Meredith.

The Todd Salem Motion Picture Studio article, long, detailed and dynamite, exploded Thursday morning, with all the back-up evidence and neutral non-accusatory wording. "A world-class investigative reporting—neutral, non-biased, just the facts and their results," Alan told Meredith. Meredith's boss Russ Talbot at *News— New York* had the firm's legal team vet every word in Meredith's text before the story ran.

She was at the TV studio for her weekly appearance when the article, wired to newspapers all over the country, was published. On Raymond's advice, she sent everyone out of the house for the day— out of caution—Riley at school then Gloria's house along with Lupe. Raymond was at work and then in an unmarked car across the street until it seemed safe to re-enter the house later in the evening. Ivan had remained with Alan until the story appeared, and seemed to be reveling in his time with veteran Hollywood player. Two senior leaders from different industries, holding court with one another. Meredith messengered a published version to Elizabeth Garten, Sal's daughter.

The most important repercussion from the news, however, was an emergency meeting of the studio partners one week later. By then the assembled group—all including every one of the venture capital partners—agreed that there be no blowback toward anyone, especially each other, and agreed to more fully investigate the contractual situation. Ivan reported confidentially to Meredith that old and revised copies were compared, the originals shown to have been altered. Reference to Sal Luck had been omitted completely. "It must have been after Sal took sick," said Ivan, "because he could—and might—have come back to revisit it any time if he was alive. No one would have taken that risk."

It was assumed Bill Pokka, an early partner no longer involved, had engineered the fraudulent documents, the forged signatures—with the unwitting help of a paralegal at his firm. Pokka's company was morphed eventually into Bob Sands' organization and Pokka was no longer to be found in the fifty states—the paralegal, at work in San Francisco, unaware that she'd been involved in anything wrong to remove Sal Luck. She was devastated because she was a huge fan of his work. Further investigation was in play by local and federal law enforcement.

And Ivan was assured the two rude men who'd visited his home early one morning to talk about the studio deal, were legit members of the venture capital firm. Just not very affable ones. Or lawyers. Ivan had recommended they stay in the office behind their computers.

☆☆☆

As Meredith came off the set of the morning talk show a week later, she was greeted by a well-presented Asian man introducing himself as Darren Ho, a member of the partnership of Chinese investors within the Frogner VC group of San Francisco—new partners in the Silicon Valley studio. Still, wrapped in her audio wires and broadcast make-up, she invited him back to the set, not willing to be alone with him in her normal dressing area. She asked Cassie to join them. Ho was pleasant, affable and funny, spoke with no accent, and seemed comfortable in the situation. More than either Meredith or Cassie could admit.

"Look," he told them, "I understand. You're certainly not the first to bring up the worry about Chinese investment in technology, movies … " And went on to talk about viable investments globally, productive partnerships, citing worldwide examples. He told them he had graduated Suma Cum Laude from Wharton School of Business, understood and respected—upheld—American financial beliefs and standards. The two women nodded and took it in. Meredith jotted down a few notes, although her microphone was still live, so every word was recorded. Concluding the brief discussion, the journalist directed Ho to the International correspondent at *News—New York*. He reluctantly took the information, seemingly disappointed by the handoff.

As she and Cassie recapped after the tall, slim man left, "There's probably something to run, but not much that wasn't a beautifully sculpted non-statement with no real new information or viewpoints … " Meredith assessed.

"But he sure was great looking," mused Cassie. "Great smile—great butt." The episode was over. The story, as far as Meredith would take it, wrapped. Other journalists would have to pick up tailings as the world economy evolved.

★ ★ ☆

Another mandatory meeting of the movie studio partners and their legal team two weeks after the story ran revealed the contractual indiscretions. In keeping with the original contracts, and avoiding costly litigation, the group voted to compensate Sal Luck's heirs for rents received from the lease of the Milpitas property to the Todd Salem Motion Picture Partners. And appropriate income and other benefits from future revenues of the studio partners.

A month later, under a November sky—troubled and spongy—Meredith pulled into the parking lot of the Sportsman's Lodge, a San Fernando Valley mainstay for business executives and local celebrity dining. She was shown to a large round table where Ivan and Alan were already seated, chattering and laughing. A very good pairing, thought Meredith.

Then Elizabeth Luck, her grandson and a younger woman—Meredith assumed was Elizabeth's nurse daughter—Sal Luck's granddaughter. Lunch conversation flowed, food was served. As the meal progressed, the old electronics pioneer reached over and lightly kissed Meredith's cheek. "Thank you," he murmured. She looked at him quizzically. "I may be rumored to be rich, and famous in a different world than yours, Meredith. But I still have integrity and a sense of both values and consequences. The Maker always wins. So, your tenacity helped us come to terms of this terrible oversight. And it's time for Sal Luck to be recognized, even this long after he's been gone."

"He's not gone," mused Meredith. "Look around—he's everywhere in this group. And over there—in that little boy."

The lunch dishes were being collected and guests prepared to leave. Ivan stood up to bid goodbye to the Luck family with some quiet private comments. They'd obviously spent some time together before the lunch. All were smiling. Salvatore waved enthusiastically as they made their way out of the room.

"I have another announcement," Ivan beamed as he returned

to the table. His round face wrinkled mischievously. "I'm supposedly semi-retired—about ten years. But now it's total and final. I'm devoting my time to writing not only my own story, but so many stories of the amazing journey through the development of the computer industry. I have a few of those stories in my arsenal as you might imagine!"

Alan looked down at his coffee. Meredith turned and listened closely. "My good friend Alan Jaymar will work with me," Ivan continued. "Maybe he can make me into the kind of literary celebrity he developed over so many decades … or at least get me published." Meredith lifted her water glass in salute.

As the group disbursed, she huddled with Alan. "You've really bitten off a lot this time," she chided him. "I thought you'd retired."

"I did," he said. "But what an opportunity to learn new things, work with someone who is more than a pretty face or an image on a screen." He chortled. "Potty's slipping and I'm antsy. It's time for something of a challenge."

"Well, you're always up for that, Alan. Remember how you and your assistant totally wrote the poetry of that hippie guy out of San Francisco—published three volumes for him and sold millions of books. And made him into a celebrity—and rich." Both friends laughed out loud.

"What's next, Meredith?" asked Ivan who had just joined the twosome and lit up one of his seedy cigars retrieved from his pants pocket.

"Deadline on Thursdays, just … well, the usual," she sighed. "Probably nothing so complex or robust or interesting as the Todd Salem Motion Picture Studio story … "

"But life, Hollywood and computers, just keep on keepin' on," said Ivan. "What convinced you to pursue our studio with such determination and detail?" he asked.

"I know a good story when I see one," she smiled.

As Ivan told Meredith, the Silicon Valley has expanded throughout the world—as has Hollywood. Filmmakers/ innovators like Tyler Perry found their own home territory—his in Georgia—and took a piece of "Hollywood" with him. In recent years, cities, states and other entities have established their own production centers to accommodate and attract film companies. The state of Hawaii has begun developing a major production facility in conjunction with the University of Hawaii on West Oahu. Experts say that without a full-capacity film production entity, global producers think of Hawaii only for "location" work in the verdant natural settings, but don't stay to complete a project for lack of state-of-the-art technical support. The author recalls members of the original *Hawaii Five 0 cast* commenting that interior shooting frequently came to a halt when rain splattered on the tin roofing of the "studio."

Recently, Las Vegas announced the development of its own film center. *The Los Angeles Times* reported the negative economic impact on L.A.'s traditional filmland business community as producers move their projects into other cities where it costs less to work.

Early Legwoman content readers Jim and Nancy Vincler strongly contributed to this story. Their San Francisco Bay area business, Vincler Communication, has been teaching Silicon Valley engineers and techs how to translate jargon into regular-people English for decades. Jim, a former military investigator, investigative journalist and early Silicon Valley newspaper editor recalled in an industry blog how Silicon Valley was named.

"The name Silicon Valley was popularized by newspaperman Don Hoefler in 1971. Don was a columnist for *Electronic News* (*EN*), a weekly tabloid that covered the electronics industry. *EN* landed on the desks of electronics industry executives and managers on Monday mornings. These people did not start their work week before reading *EN*. They wanted to know what was being said about the people, the products, and the companies in the industry. *EN* was the Bible. If a story didn't appear in *EN*, it didn't happen.

Don was working for several weeks on a story about how the semiconductor industry blossomed in the Santa Clara Valley during the Sixties. One day a couple of marketing guys called Don and said they were going to be in San Francisco that day and invited him to lunch. I worked with Don as a reporter for *EN* and tagged along. During the lunch conversation, one guy said something about "Silicon Valley." I saw Don's eyes subtly light up like a poker player who had just filled a straight, as he asked, "Silicon Valley? Where'd that come from?"

The marketing manager said, "Oh, that's what the guys call it." We shared our amusement about the moniker that the industry sales people had created and then went on to other topics.

On our walk back to the office, I said to Don, "Cool name, huh?" He smiled.

When we got back to the office, Don, who was wrapping up his story, changed the title and wired it to *EN* headquarters in New York. The next Monday his story appeared with the bold headline: SILICON VALLEY, U.S.A.: computerhistory.org/revolution/digital-logic/12/328/1401

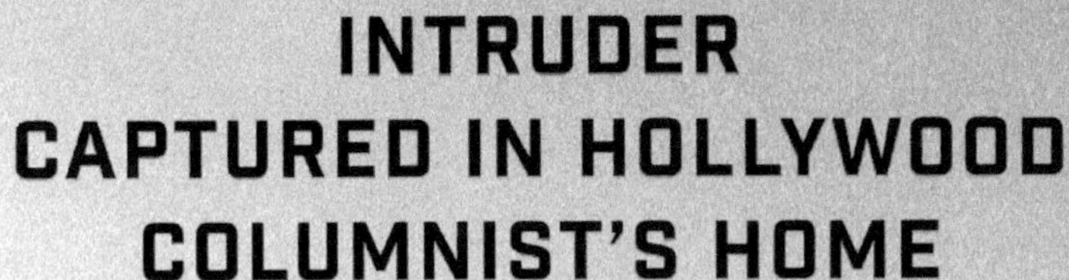
INTRUDER
CAPTURED IN HOLLYWOOD
COLUMNIST'S HOME
1996

1996
INTRUDER CAPTURED IN
HOLLYWOOD COLUMNIST'S HOME

Cat on Ice

He couldn't understand what he was seeing through the veranda glass door into the house. The big man who took care of things seemed to be sleeping on the floor near the kitchen. T.K.—the human—rarely ever slept anywhere but in the bed upstairs—with "M" (called Meredith by the humans), the other primary inhabitant of the place. M was away for the day. With the small tyke who belonged to them. And T.K. was crumpled onto the floor in his running clothes—shorts and t-shirt. A visor, now lying next to his head. Eyes closed.

But Paco's heightened sensory system already baffled and on alert, sensed the presence of an unfamiliar someone in the house— filtered sounds vaguely wafting from the second story—a slightly pernicious odor. Most ears and noses probably wouldn't have noticed them.

Paco quickly reviewed his morning which started off normally. He had loped along the sand-side perimeter of the dozen homes strung on the beach enroute to his own homeplace—not quite a melody but a rhythmic cadence in his step—in his very heartbeat. California sunshine—and an energetic and bright day at the beach. And around the household doors and garden of his neighbors.

Mrs. Melley had put out a fresh bowl of water. The Sinclair twins—eight years old—left some treats for him on the step. He slipped quickly by the Targon's house. Mr. Targon hated cats. And Paco had made an outward curve around the Williams gate because Mrs. Williams was allergic. But bless Marty Villa for always leaving tuna scraps for him.

Paco knew to make the circle tour at first light, past and then back through his neighbors' homes. Otherwise, some other visitor would reap the good nature and generosity of his friends. He had stopped to enjoy his treat, then settling into the sunshine on the walkway for a moment to lick his fur clean. He scanned the scene with his wary eyes, looking for his household companion, T.K., his usual beach-explorer partner, the only other male human, in the family.

Paco hadn't caught sight of his sturdy moving silhouette anywhere along the beach. The sleek grey cat roused himself from his cursory grooming, rearranged his limbs and proceeded to trek warily home, his intuitive curiosity in high gear. Most Saturdays and Sunday, the big human launched from the house into a jog that took him about four miles—a trip he said was for renewed vigor and good health. He usually arrived home about the same time as the feline, often climbing the veranda stairs simultaneously.

The two beach runners lived in a three story house on Malibu Beach, the human with his companion, "Meredith," "M" to Paco, the cat's original and only housemate. Twelve years ago, T.K. came, a tall, stoic detective who helped M find the killer of her famous gossip columnist boss, a tragic drama accelerating M into high celebrity status of her own which Paco willingly accompanied his human.

Now, Paco was a vital and energetic "middle-ager" like his "M," although he knew she'd never admit to middle age. The relationship with T.K. was not as organic.

Paco initially shunned the congenial detective, the interloper, then hazed him, believing nothing establishes territory like a rich aromatic dump into a shiny loafer, or a good piss on boxer shorts left in a heap on the floor outside the shower. Eventually, a truce evolved, as T.K. learned the cat's menu preferences, to honor his prominent standing atop whatever refrigerator occupied the kitchen. And his undisputed first place in the heart of M.

Now, Paco slunk silently through a discreet cat door into the kitchen and crept along the walls to where the detective was sprawled, unmoving. Neither seeing nor hearing another human in the room, the cat sniffed around the detective, placed his slightly damp nose against the man's face to feel the essence. Relieved he felt a strong sense of life in the forehead, Paco quickly took in the sensory essence of the house. The kitchen had been uncharacteristically messed up—refrigerator door left open, crumbs and remnants of a corn chip box on the floor, an empty beer bottle overturned as well. Bu the real focus was on the upstairs where the cat could hear rapid movement, a few "clunks" on the floor and an occasional grumble. He intuited that nothing happening on the second floor was normal or good. M said Paco had a sixth sense for trouble. That must be it, he reasoned and silently slipped up the stairs, hunkered deeply close to the carpet.

Peering warily into the large, main bedroom, he saw a weather-worn figure pawing through M's dressing table, pulling items from the cosmetic drawers, her cherished jewelry box upended, bracelets and earrings, necklaces and hair gems scattered on the tabletop, spilling onto the floor. Paco smiled slyly, knowing that the "good" stuff" was kept in a hidden safe where the riff raff would never find it. But still, Paco recognized some of the decorative pieces M wore to movie premieres and fancy parties. His anger pulsated but he kept it under control. He knew danger when confronted with it!

He regarded the intruder carefully, recognizing him from recent beach sightings. Youngish with long, limp, grimy blondish hair—messy from too many days and nights in the ocean elements—scabby face and a nose that was unhealthily crooked, torn t-shirt and ragged shorts that hadn't seen detergent in months, no shoes. And an odor that Paco had intuited from the veranda.

Paco's laser-like golden eyes quickly scanned the room for a piece of metal hardware like the one T.K. often carried as a policeman—and kept locked up to make sure no one else ever touched it. Saw nothing, but noticed a long piece of thick metal with a claw at one end. The kind of rod that would normally frighten the feline into a quick exit and into hiding.

But a slight, subtle rustling from downstairs emboldened Paco who glanced furtively from a corner of the highest step. The downed T.K. was stirring, struggling to sit up, shaking his head to clear it. The feline knew the big human would handle the intruder. T.K. had swiftly dispatched other trespassers who had violated the boundaries of the family abode at least twice before over the years.

But the subtle rousing from below also caught the attention of the interloper who rushed to the top of the stairs, crowbar now in hand, intent on protecting his newly purloined turf. He launched himself into a reckless descent, and Paco's instinct propelled him forward into the gaggle of legs haphazardly navigating the steps. Both cat and scavenger stumbled then tumbled in a messy heap down the perilous stairwell amid obscenities and expletives and feline screeches, landing unceremoniously at the bottom. Paco streaked away and lodged himself under a sofa, the intruder sprawled inert, unmoving.

T.K. pulled himself vertical, assessing the noisy drama crashing around him. Still shaking the muddle from his head, he recognized the unmoving figure heaped at the bottom of the stairwell. Groping along the island counter, into a slender cabinet door with no visible latch, T.K. adroitly manipulated the sly cupboard which sprang open. He reached deep into the space, quickly fingered an unseen keypad, extracting a small handgun.

Turning quicky to the downed thief, he gulped in a breath of relief. The figure remained motionless on the floor. Pointing the weapon with guarded motion, he placed his fingers on the neck and found a pulse. Carefully rearranging hands and binding them and the man's ankles with kitchen twine, T.K. slid over to the phone and dialed 911. The conversation was brief but pointed.

Then the big detective sat down in one of the leather recliners, dropped his head in his hands and took a few big breaths. Two wide round eyes peered at him from under the sofa and then the whole cat crawled out ever so slowly and cautiously. He glanced at the bound-up beach bum, looked at T.K.. "Opened the door, ready to run but left my visor in the bathroom," the human explained to the cat. "Went to get it—the guy ran in and hit me with my own tire iron!"

Man and cat shared a moment of focused acknowledgment before the large grey feline levitated to the kitchen counter and then to the top of the refrigerator where he sat imperiously.

"Nice moves, by the way!" the detective admonished just as the shrill police siren arrived at the house, and the prone bandit began to wriggle on the floor. T.K. stood up, saluted the cat and went to the front door. Paco sat Sphinx-like tall on the refrigerator for two or three seconds, then folded fluidly into a complex figure eight and licked his tail.

HONOLULU CONFIDENTIAL'S LAST SEASON?

1996

1999
HONOLULU CONFIDENTIAL'S
LAST SEASON?

Honolulu-Kona Coast, Hawaii

"Ed died." The voice was flat, emotionless. T.K. Raymond recognized it as that of his half-brother Tad Oakley, and the message was one they'd both anticipated but dreaded since learning of one another 's existence two years earlier. The man who had raised Tad, his grandfather, had passed on.

"I'm sorry, Tad. So sorry. I only met your grandad that one time, but I envied you for having him and all he brought to you. Can I do anything?"

"Nah," came the sluggish response from Tad. "I'm bummed, but he'd had heart problems for a long time so not surprised."

"Funeral or service? Wichita?" Raymond asked.

"Two weeks out," Tad replied. "I'm going. There'll be some issues to sort out. He and my uncle Sid did some important planning so the property and wills—stuff like that—are already taken care of. I'll have some paperwork to do … " A heavy silence came across the line. Raymond—sitting in his West Los Angeles special unit investigation office; Oakley—in the software development company offices in Irvine, California, fifty miles south.

"Want me to go with you?" Raymond asked, sincerity edged with uncertainty and question. The two had a most uncertain history together.

"Un … no, I don't think so," Tad answered very quietly. "I

think I have to tell the 'big secret' to the rest of the family now that Ed's gone. And that will be rocky." Tad's secret was that while they shared a common father, whose life-long partner/spouse had been Raymond's mother, Tad's mother had been a beautiful young actress whose body was found murdered in the California desert only two years before, but some twenty years after her death. T.K. Raymond learned of her existence and relationship with his father only then. And only then met his half-brother, Tad. They had agreed never to tell the sordid truth to the actress's father, Tad's grandfather, who raised the boy and believed his daughter had died a Hollywood star, of pneumonia.

Telling "the secret" meant honestly laying out the truth to Tad's uncle and nephews who, like Grandpa Ed, still thought two-year-old Tad had been brought to the family by a grieving husband who claimed he could not care for the boy alone. And who then disappeared into Mexico. Through Raymond's exhaustive investigation of the actress's death, he learned about his father's affair and the family loosely connected to him through Tad.

"My mother was kind of a mythological princess—went off to Hollywood, made movies, married a big timer and then died tragically of pneumonia. Uncle Sid, especially, really fantasized her. His 'beloved' sister."

"I'm sorry, Tad. Really, anything I can help with? Are you okay?"

"I guess so," came the younger man's voice. He slumped forward on his desk and fingered the small Rubik's cube in front of him. A shock of his brown hair fell across his forehead. His eyes were deep pools of stress. The trip back to Wichita would not be easy. "I'm going to take a couple of weeks off," he said. "The time's good—things here are quiet. I need some place to work this out."

"We knew it would come," Raymond reminded.

"Doesn't make it any easier. You went through all your anxiety and trauma finding out about my mother-and your father—two years ago. Now, it's my turn."

"Our father, and the truth is not under the carpet," snuffed

Raymond. "It'll probably sit with me forever. We never could tell my mother about it. She knew about the affair, and about you. But not that I'd found you and what had happened to your mother. My mother thought your mother married my dad's business partner and lived happily ever after."

Murmurs and pauses across the line until Raymond spoke up. "Hey, if you're taking extra time off, why don't you stay with us here on the beach for a few days. Nice change of pace ... quiet place to think and reflect ... "

Tad mumbled and finally said, "It sounds great right now. Let me call you back on it." The two disengaged. Raymond wondered if there was, at all, anything he could do to honorably mark the passing of the kind old gentleman who raised Tad Oakley.

★★☆

"You seem quiet—pensive—tonight," Meredith mentioned to Raymond as they cleaned up the dinner dishes. The sound of the TV chattering from the family room where seven-year-old Riley was watching a game show.

"Tad called today," Raymond explained. "His grandfather, Ed, passed away. Kind of caught me unprepared."

"Sorry, Raymond," Meredith responded, closing the dishwasher. She sat down on one of the kitchen island stools and patted the one next to her, beckoning Raymond to join her. "What happened?" she asked, pouring him a glass of red wine from the decorative bottle on the counter, and one for herself. Her tall, silver-haired husband lowered himself onto the stool with a sigh.

"Had the audacity to get old. I know the feeling today. But, he had a heart condition that had followed him around for a long time. Heart attack yesterday morning."

"I know you kind of bonded with him when you were looking into the murder of his daughter—the actress ... "

"Tad's mother," Raymond finished the thought.

"But … well, … will you go to Wichita with Tad?"

Raymond shook his head. "Neither Ed nor his other child, his son Sid, knew the full story. Tad and I agreed that for his grandfather's sake, we would never upend the picture they all carried about how she died, married happily, with her son Tad. How he came to live with them."

"Now Tad wants to make things right for his uncle and cousins?"

"Tired of keeping the confidence. Too big of a secret."

Meredith nodded, wondering how the family might take the news. She looked at Raymond. "Kind of like keeping it from your mom. She still believes the actress married your father's partner Mal Odenato who moved mother and child to Mexico with him." Raymond nodded.

"Except now it's not such a burden," he muttered, "because well … mom doesn't even recognize me. So, any story she hears won't mean anything." Meredith reached over to put her hand on his cheek.

"When's the funeral?"

"Two weeks. I invited him to spend some time here afterward. He wanted some distance and has time off."

Meredith stared into her glass. "That's the time I will be in Honolulu for a couple of days—the every-couple-of-years visit to the TV shows shooting there," she said quietly. "You'd be here with Tad by yourselves—except for Riley. But Lola is coming to visit and relieve her aunt Lupe for 10 days. You guys could have a good visit with Riley under the tutelage of Lola."

Raymond scowled, puzzled. "I didn't know Lola was still around here. I thought she went off to Santa Barbara to work after she graduated and left us—and handed us over to Générale Lupe."

"Lola's taking a vacation of her own and figured free rent on Malibu Beach was a pretty nice idea. She'll probably be a lot easier on you than Lupe—and keep Riley a lot more engaged. More private time for you and Tad."

Raymond thought about the idea, said he'd talk with his half-brother then sat pensively, staring into his wine. The quiet of the evening moved in, along with the surf outside. Meredith watched Raymond's face, mired in a cloud of concern, reached out and pulled on his hand. "There's one way to push away the blues," she grinned flirtatiously. He looked at her, put down his glass and followed her upstairs to the bedroom.

"Sleep is over-rated," she murmured as they dropped onto the big bed.

But another unexpected change developed. Four days before Meredith's departure for Hawaii, Raymond sat down opposite her on the kitchen island. She was just sipping her cup of coffee, alone, before the phones began to ring or her assistant arrived. Riley had left for school, riding with a classmate. Lupe was upstairs working. She wondered why Raymond had not left for his office. She looked at him, curious.

"I wanted to spend a couple of minutes to tell you about something I did without talking to you first," he began, a pallor of guilt and hesitation washed on his face.

Oh, oh, she thought. Sounds serious—maybe ominous. "What?" she pushed.

"Wasn't exactly smart—but at the time it seemed like the right thing to do," he cautioned.

She nodded. "And … "

"I booked Tad and I into Kona while you're in Honolulu. Then, I hoped you'd come over and spend 3 days with us."

She shook her head, confused. "What … ? Why? And what about Riley? She'll be here alone or are you thinking of bringing her with you? I'm puzzled. Help me out." If she put in the effort, she couldn't really screw her face into confusion any more than it was.

Raymond sat tall and explained without rancor or apology. "Tad has had a very upending series of personal events in the past two years. They've rattled him—the truth of his mother AND father, her death and well … me, a half-brother. And now the death of his grandfather who raised him in such a loving way … I thought maybe having a couple of beers with Juan Medieros … well, he always seems to be on solid ground … ”

“And … a double conversation with Juan might be helpful for the half-brother as well … who seems a little taken aback by the latest developments … ” Meredith added, not quite cynically, inwardly thinking of how much pleasure and reality Juan, their protestant minister friend on the Big Island of Hawaii always brought to the couple. The minister who conducted the irreverent marriage ceremony seven years earlier. Since then, Juan, his wife Celi, Raymond and Meredith had socialized many times. Sometimes in Hawaii, several times when the Island couple had visited at the Malibu house. Interaction had always been light-hearted and enjoyable, but also delved into deep subjects and conversational hills and valleys that left everyone feeling fulsome but grounded.

Raymond sat steadfast and gazed at Meredith. “I’ve already spoken with Lola AND Lupe AND Gloria,” he referred to Meredith’s closest friend. “They’re in unison and cahoots. Riley won’t hardly miss us.” He waited for her response.

“Do you need me in this endeavor?” she asked, knowing he was right about the team that would be caring for their seven year old daughter, also taken by surprise that he had already knitted the group together.

He laughed. “I always need you—and I wouldn’t dare venture into Kona Village without you in my thatched hut. Tad’s on his own in his own room there! And I’ve already thought about Riley missing school and coming along. But, I’m not ready—yet—to surrender our own personal halo that’s around the place to her small, persistent voice. So, Lola has agreed to dedicate four of her days here to being one hundred percent at her disposal. Riley’ll be in school three of them. Lupe will spend the evenings with the two of them, and Gloria will take Riley to the aquarium with Trey one afternoon. And Lola swears she’ll keep her focused on homework and maybe a burger down the road.” His gaze stayed on Meredith’s face, making the importance of the plan clear.

She thought about the island idyll—a large isolated salad of lush tropical growth ringing a seductive lagoon, thatched hales—or huts, outfitted with Polynesian décor but modern amenities, and no phones, televisions or radios allowed. One pay phone available in the lobby area. A jaunty, affable bar built into a beached, wrecked boat, and gourmet food, wines and delicacies from an open-air dining room. Perfect recipe for a true get-away from civilization. A couple of days in that solitude sounded very nice, if a little worrisome.

"Okay," she agreed, realizing this was not just important, but mandatory. She could only imagine how much sorrow and disarray the two brothers were feeling. "As long as we have Riley well cared for." Meredith always worked first and foremost to make sure their daughter was on solid ground and not dangling away from her parents' often eclectic and peripatetic professions. This time, Meredith realized, she had some fast organizational work to do before she would feel comfortable heading for Honolulu.

Two weeks—and then some—later, she was bouncing through the heavily forested jungle of Oahu, on Hawaii's North Shore, in an ATV, after observing the filming of *Hawaii Confidential*. The detective series was well into its fifth year, following on the heels of the legendary *Hawaii Five-0* and *Magnum P.I. Confidential's* popularity had never been as strong as the two predecessors, but the scenery, location uniqueness plus a drop-dead gorgeous male star, Brent Silver, made it a popular watch for many. And Meredith agreed to visit and write about the show primarily because of her friendship with the series' publicist Molly Moore.

The journalist had spent several hours sitting uncomfortably in the overly-used seats of the open vehicle and in a series of hard folding metal chairs, surrounded by the hive of filming activity. She was gripped by a sense of surreal daydreaming. Her trip was to have been a short, two days in and out with a few interviews at the Honolulu studio or a nearby restaurant. Instead, the schedule had changed the week before her arrival and the cast and crew were working in the wilds. Talk was in the cramped trailer of the star, or the open-air gathering place with the producer who confided in Meredith that the show was probably in its last season. She wasn't surprised but felt sad that the wonderous location would again be without a resident TV show. She convinced the producer to let her "leak"—suggest—cancellation might be in the works. It was a good story and made the trip worthwhile.

Dinner the night before was a hurried conversation with the one actor who was a hold-over from the former *Magnum P.I.* series. Fortunately, the meeting took place at one of the Islands more venerable hotels, the New Otani Kaimana Beach, on the lanai of the bar-grill. And that choice was because filming earlier in the day had been at the extensive and verdant Queen Kapiolani Park across the road from the hotel. She'd also snagged breakfast with the woman who ran the local film festival and who had a long history with Hollywood filming in Hawaii. That interview gave Meredith the credible edge to the usual reporting from a production location. The hotel was also where Meredith was staying for her two days on Oahu. As always, she tried to arrange her activities as efficiently as possible. The days of extending an out-of-town work trip to sight-see or visit friends were long gone. Especially with a seven-year-old in the house.

Returning from the afternoon's work and before dinner, Meredith called home. When her good friend Gloria answered the phone instead of Lola, it immediately worried Meredith. "Where's Lola? Is everything all right there?"

Gloria just laughed. "Yes. I just got here but Lola was on her way up the stairs with Riley to send her to sleep—it's three hours later here. She's there now and says to tell you 'it's all okay. Riley's had a great day.' I stopped by to drop off her sweater she left in my car at the aquarium. How's your trip going?"

Meredith snarked, "Fine for now. Tomorrow's not so wonderful. We're forging into the wilderness. I didn't bring clothes to be gunking around the jungle and mud in an ATV. And, I feel like I've written this story with different names too many times before." Gloria clucked her sympathy.

"But—" her friend went on, "then I found the diamond in the costume-jeweled trip. An unusual story that bathes the trip in a nice, worthwhile, glow, Coming back from the park, I noticed this guy going down the sidewalk of the main street. He was pushing a … marimba, I guess. All by himself and just muscling it along the sidewalk like he was on a mission. He dropped a little notebook and I walked over to help him pick it up. I thought I recognized him. I felt so silly.

"Aren't you Arthur Lyman?' I asked. Sounded like a preteen. Gloria, do you remember Arthur Lyman?"

"Yellow Bird," chuckled Gloria. "And all those exotica albums. Drums and bird calls. I studied to them … day-dreamed to them," she reminisced over the phone line from an ocean away.

"Remember when we were in college and came here to Honolulu for a student conference of some kind, we splurged and went to see him at the Dome theater at the Hawaiian Village Hotel."

Gloria practically gasped. "Gawd, yes. That music was soo hypnotic and he was sooo handsome."

"Still is. I interrupted his walk to ask him what he was doing with his xylophone or marimba or whatever on a busy sidewalk," a giant smile bubbled in Meredith voice as she told the story. "We must have talked for a half hour, in the humidity and sunshine, there on the busy street. He told me that he still has records—re-releases and stuff—that sell. There has been a couple of resurgences in the 'beach' music' craze—but in his retirement, he plays—all by himself—at the New Otani Hotel. He loves making music. But they don't have storage for his … marimba? Anyhow—he stores it a few blocks down the street. He pushes the huge instrument after his gig—must be good exercise. I'm sorry I missed his daily show."

"You always seem to find the best stories, Merri. Sometimes I'd like to just follow you around for a day. I look forward to reading that one."

"It's kind of the highlight of the trip," chuckled the journalist. "Everything else is—well, humdrum. Of course, pretty and highlighted with the lilt of the tropics but—business as usual. Arthur Lyman—well, very special. You're sure all is well with the gang there?"

"Lola just yelled she'll talk to you tomorrow and Riley says 'hugs and kisses.'"

The *Confidential* schedule revision meant that the next day, Meredith no longer had time to change clothes after her set-side interviews in the jungle and a rushed trip to the airport in time to catch her flight. Rain had muddied the pathways, evidence of which streaked her pants and a few hidden places on arms and neck. Well, she shrugged, stuffing her notes and materials into her shoulder bag, it wasn't as if anyone expected her to step off the plane in perfect fashion. Jeans and a t-shirt would have to do.

Now, bumping along the paths from the remote filming site for *Honolulu Confidential,* she felt her thoughts meld into the cadence of the ATV's momentum. Amid the compacted arranging of carpools to school, Gloria's schedule to take the kids to the aquarium, the arrival of Lola—who had to re-familiarize herself with the household schedule and rules—many new since she'd left two years before. Packing for a short work trip was usually simple for Meredith, who'd done it so often before. Travel basics were always ready to slide into the suitcase, work clothes for the "road" always set aside and ready to fold. And usually when she was way, Raymond was home along with Lupe, the house-helper, who, between them, kept Riley on a normal, unremarkable schedule. For this journey, however, by the time Meredith had managed the household and Riley's needs, her own work, and her own travel arrangements plus overseeing Raymond's, double-checking on Tad's, she was exhausted just arriving at the Honolulu airport.

But a full night's sleep in a pleasant hotel room devoid of typical noises and demands usually gave her rest. Her two nights at the New Otani did, in fact, mellow and energize her. Whenever she was on the set of any movie or TV production, no matter how mundane the interviews and subject, she felt the fascination and high that had lured her to the show business field in the first place. And her breakfast with the founder of the film festival for the state brought her both energy and pleasure.

She loved this part of her work. On the short flight to the Kona Coast, she drifted into a nap thinking about the early shows like *Hawaiian Eye* with Robert Conrad and Connie Stevens—and even a season with Troy Donahue—in the late 50s and early 60s. And the many years of the radio show *Hawaii Calls* that only made it to TV for one year in 1965-66. There were also thousands of movies and television shows filmed at least in part around Oahu and other neighboring islands. Some, Meredith had traveled to cover for her columns. Her reverie was bumped back to reality when the plane landed at the verdant Kona Airport.

She collected her carryon bag from the overhead bin, slung her work bag that held her purse and materials, over her shoulder and headed out into the balmy sunlight. The small regional airport on Hawaii's largest and southern-most island always welcomed visitors with a lilting floral fragrance they seldom forget. Meredith stepped off the stairs from the aircraft and walked briskly into the small terminal. She looked around expecting to see Raymond. But she recognized no one. She gazed around and walked toward the entrance of the building. Suddenly Juan Medeiros ran toward her, almost panting.

"So sorry, I was supposed to be here fifteen minutes ago, but I got a phone call … "

"Where's Raymond and Tad?" she puzzled, looking around.

"Come on," the swarthy minister beckoned. "I'm your ride and on the way to the resort, I'll explain why you have me as your driver." Meredith's friendship with the local man pushed away most of her concern. But usually, Raymond was the one who showed up unexpectedly, and always when anticipated.

Juan placed her bags in the back seat of his Jeep and as she secured a seat belt, he pulled out of the parking lot. "Comfortable?" he asked.

"Sure," she added looking around at the green ground covers sprouting from hard black volcanic rocks.

"So, we have a situation right now," Juan began. Meredith turned, settling into her seat, to watch him. "You know that Tad's grandfather died a couple of weeks ago." Meredith nodded. "And Tad went to Wichita for the funeral, to finalize whatever details needed signatures and stuff?"

"Uh-huh," she murmured.

"Well, he sat down with his Uncle Sid Oakley and told him the truth about his mother's—Sid's sister's—death. You know the whole story, and that no one had told any of the Oakley family anything about the actual situation in which Tad was born and his mother lived and died until the grandfather passed—last week." Again, Meredith nodded.

"Uncle Sid and his family were pretty much in shock when they heard about it."

"Tad only told them because he wanted them to know the full story, after grandfather, Ed, passed away," Meredith interjected. "Until that time, no one wanted Ed to be hurt or upset."

"Well, Sid was first shocked. The whole family was, of course. Then he sank into pretty heavy grief. And that turned into anger and blame. Tad had flown home to California and to meet up with T.K. for the trip here. Sid turned his rage toward Tad and T.K. He'd never even met T.K. But just felt like someone needed to 'pay' and since T.K.'s father—he kind of forgot the man was also Tad's father—was the evil-doer, T.K. should bear the responsibility of the lie. And the murder—well, all of it. Sid arrived here totally unexpectedly to confront them late last night. Last flight from Honolulu."

Meredith stared out the Jeep's window, watching the dark, Mars-like scenery pass, trying to imagine what had transpired in the serene lagoon-side resort for the past 18 hours. "No one told me. I talked with Raymond last night," she replied. "But earlier in the evening, I guess."

Juan nodded. "No one knew what to say or do. T.K. called me over to the hotel about eleven. Sid only arrived about ten and he was already hyped up and primed for a confrontation, started in ranting, loud and toxic accusations. Then breaking into weeping. Totally manic. T.K. managed to tone him down, but you could practically touch the adrenalin pumping through Sid. We all spent hours talking to him. He was exhausted and a mess. Who wouldn't be? Carrying that much emotional baggage all the way across the country and then the Pacific Ocean? It seemed like one explosive outburst after another."

"What's he doing now?"

"Pacing, sleeping some of the day. Snarling during others. He's in Tad's beach hut, and we don't know what will be next, but the guys decided to stay close." Meredith shuddered with the news and fought to stay focused.

"How'd he know where to find Tad?"

"Apparently, he called your home and because he said he was family, your babysitter told him. She didn't realize what he had in mind." Meredith took a deep troubled breath. They were rolling down the narrow road through the lava field into the lush area where the exotic resort sat. The two left the car. Juan carried her small suitcase, and they trudged into the open-air lobby. "We'll go to Raymond's—sorry, your and Raymond's—hut and see what the situation is now."

They wended their way through the lush pathways between the thatched cottages, tall coconut palms lining the flagstones, thick tropical hibiscus and other bushes adding their soft whispers to the quiet slushing of the surf beyond. They passed through the outdoor lobby, empty now save for numerous orchid plants tall and graceful and the receptionist, blossom tucked behind her ear, who greeted Meredith with a huge smile. Although smiling in return, Meredith felt her own sense of anger building. In some way, she felt her own home had been violated. As the path rounded and opened onto a swath of beach, she saw the three men sitting silently around a small table on the front lanai of a hut or as it was called in Kona Village "hale (hah-lay). As Juan guided her toward the one next door, she figured it was Tad's room.

"Let me see what's going on," Juan instructed. "Stay here until I know the mood." She nodded, tossing her bag on the Hawaiian quilt that covered the bed in the well-appointed suite, heavy in tropical woods, textures and décor. She sat down heavily in a rattan chair and called the home number, still a little unaccustomed to carrying a phone. It had only become a part of the day-to-day life a couple of years before. "Hello, Meredith?" She recognized the hesitant voice of Lola.

Greeting the lovely young woman who'd been part of their household for four years and was back as a substitute and partner for her aunt now, Meredith could sense an emotional tone. "I'm so sorry, Meredith," the young voice blurted.

"What's going on, Lola. We talked yesterday and all seemed fine. Is it Riley?"

"No," growled the youthful voice. "She's great—I wanted to call you back yesterday but I knew you were working out in the jungles, and well … "

"Lola, it's okay. Just tell me what happened."

"A terribly rude man phoned here night before last and said he was an uncle and was looking for Tad. Stupid, stupid of me, I told him where he was … " Meredith could hear the panic and humble fear. "And then he called T.K. a bunch of names, and me a stupid bitch … and … "

"Lola, Lola," Meredith interrupted. "Sh-h. Calm down. We have him right here and under control. I'm the one who's sorry— that you had to go through that. You're such a wonderful gem for us, and we love you as part of our family. Sid will never bother you again. Please take a deep breath and enjoy the rest of your stay. Tell Lupe all is well, and we'll see you both on Friday. Please." She felt like she was begging. Lola seemed to do as she was directed—took a deep breath and suddenly became the mature young adult Meredith knew her to be.

Still, Meredith billowed with hurt and anger for Lola. And for Tad and T.K. and for herself for not anticipating something—she couldn't have known what—but the situation in Wichita had to have been volatile.

Talking lastly with Riley, hearing the little girl recount her day with enthusiasm, helped her mood. She splashed water on her face, ran her fingers through her hair and went out to confront the trauma for herself.

Juan stood aside from the three men who sat, faces expressionless and unwavering. Tad worked a crossword puzzle. Raymond thumbed through a magazine. The face of Sid Oakley, totally new to her, was amidst them with an expression hard and laced with stoic indignation. He stared at the horizon. She walked up.

"Hey guys—thanks for sending Juan to retrieve me. But I didn't get my aloha hug—and I'm not willing to miss my first Kona Village cocktail. What's going on?" She turned toward Sid—seeing he was a beefy guy, a little given to fat, but clearly a strong one. She held out her hand.

"I'm Meredith," she said with a smile. "T.K.'s wife." The big man looked up at her, anger igniting his eyes, and did not reach out to meet her hand. Raymond pulled himself tall, with hard eyes, and an obvious protective stance, prepared for confrontation—maybe even violence. Tad pulled back as though there might be an explosion.

"Sid has had a very disturbing bit of news," Juan spoke up, "and he's been processing it."

"Well, how about we all go for a sunset cocktail," chirped Meredith, hoping to break the standoff she could feel had been festering for hours.

"Lady," Sid looked up at her, "your timing sucks and your husband's a pig and so's the kid."

Meredith scowled as she gazed into his eyes. "Well, everyone has their own opinion, and I think it's time to let it go." Sid rose up, his fists clenched as he thrust himself toward her.

"You don't even know what these asses did to my beautiful sister. You all should be … "

Meredith took a quick deep breath, slapped the man's face.

His eyes opened wide. He looked at her. "Get over yourself," she snarled. "None of these people knew anything about the life or the loves of your sister. Raymond was not even here but in Vietnam. Tad, of course, hadn't even been born when it all started. Ed knew nothing, and neither did you. Maybe the question you should be asking yourself if you were such a loyal and loving brother is why was that beautiful sister of yours ever allowed to go to a place like Hollywood? Why did she marry a bruiser to start with before she ever left? Why didn't someone from home care enough to know she was running around innocently in a big people's world where young beautiful girls get swallowed up. Where were you? Did you ever visit her? Give her advice? Someone told me you were the big brother. Well, you failed. And she lived the life she did, was cherished by many and fell into a big black Hollywood hole anyway. She did it all by herself and if it hadn't been Tad's dad, it probably would have been someone else. At least Tad was given a decent home with his family and had a good life there. You can say the same. So, get off the stage. Sorry we all didn't have the full story until very late and decided to let Grandpa Ed have a calm and contented last few years of his own. And you and your family with him as well. If you'd known about the whole story, you'd have been as compromised and sad as both T.K. and Tad. So, you're welcome!"

She stared down the bulbous man who just kept blinking his eyes. Juan reached out to Meredith, but she didn't move at all. Raymond and Tad both stared with wide eyes and partially open mouths.

"And don't EVER approach my home again. Not in person. Not by phone," Meredith said pleasantly. "Or I'll cut your balls off. Trust me—I mean it. And it will hurt." She turned and marched toward Raymond's hut. At the last moment, she turned back and said, "and I'm going to dinner. Anyone who wants to can come with me."

Sid Oakley stood continuing to blink as his two companions hesitantly began to rise from their chairs. Suddenly tears began running down the big man's face. He tried to control them with the back of his hand. Juan reached out and put an arm around his shoulders, Sid shrugged it off. Like someone had just awakened him from a bad dream, he shook his head back and forth and the tears coursed down his face. He looked up chastened. "I think I'll take a walk," he said and headed quickly toward the beach path.

"He okay?" asked Raymond uncertainly, rising halfway—wondering if he should follow the troubled man.

Juan grabbed Raymond's arm, holding him from following Sid. "He's finally collapsing into his own grief. Meredith forced it out. And grief is a mighty manacle. And it's easier to blame someone else until there's no one else to blame. Go to dinner with Meredith. I'll stay discreetly behind him. I have my phone in case there's a problem. But I think the crises is over."

Raymond hurried up the steps to his hale to find Meredith changing into a cool, flowing yellow-flowered sundress—the only nod to soft, Hawaiian style she had packed. She smiled at him as he came forward and engulfed her into a strong embrace, kissing her hair and then her lips. She reciprocated and melted against him. He pushed back and looked at her intensely before saying anything. Then, "Whoa. Lioness!"

"Let's get some dinner," she said. "I've been dreaming of calamari."

"I'm inviting Tad. He needs the nourishment—and the emotional support." Meredith nodded positively.

Sitting on the patio of the elegant self-contained resort, served by wait staff swishing through the tables and dressed in bright clothing, flowers in hair, large welcoming grins—soft slack-key guitar music in the background—the three family members began the awkward process of reacquainting themselves with each other after the emotional explosion that had taken place. And unfolding the soiled and gritty emotional laundry that had been dumped on them over the past 24 hours.

"How'd he get all this way? That's a huge trip from Wichita," puzzled Meredith, savoring the calamari she'd dreamed of. "I can't believe he didn't chill out with all the arrangements, layovers and long plane time. And, oh my, the expense … "

"It seems like he was so hyped up, all the stops and constant travel demands only agitated him more," Raymond murmured.

"And they're not rich but Sid does well enough that he could afford an unusual expense like an airline ticket to Hawaii," Tad said thoughtfully, then added, "We thought we were doing a favor for the family by waiting on the story," It sounded like an apology. "Ed's last few years were spent in a happy place with good memories. He lived with Sid and the kids and they all shared a sense of … well, contentment, understanding. At least that's how it seemed especially when I visited Ed or talked with him on the phone. What a cluster fuck I let happen."

Raymond shook his head, quietly countering his brother's assumption. He chewed on a small piece of his grilled fish and lifted the beer mug to his lips.

"Tad, you wrestled with the truth about your mother, her background and sad demise—by yourself without any loving support from that family—your family," snuffed Meredith, drizzling her fork through her salad.

"Don't let's forget that the source of it all was my father," said Raymond somberly. "And I've had to wrestle with that one, seeing the results of his misdeeds—and how it all played out through Odenato."

"Yeah, but you were also targeted by Odenato's evil widow and her Mexican thugs a couple of years ago," Tad reminded.

Meredith suddenly snapped to attention as she saw Juan's solid figure coming up the patio steps. "Oh oh," she said and took a deep drink of her mai-tai. Conversation stopped as the threesome watched the minister approach the table.

"Settle down, everyone," Juan said. "Sid seems to have reached the summit of anger and moved into the valley of just plain grief. I've suggested he stay at our house tonight and he wants to fly out tomorrow. We'll get him set up so no one has to feel awkward. He'd like to see you two … " the minister nodded to Raymond and Tad, "for just a few minutes at breakfast. I'll bring him over. I think this is the best course for him and you."

"Juan … " Raymond spoke up in a barely audible voice, emotion seeded in it. "I can't thank you enough. You kept the lid on for us in a terrible and volatile—maybe even violent—situation. I don't know how to thank you."

The minister smiled, irony sparkling in his eyes, and in his words. "You know you're my flock. After all, I bound together you two … " He gestured toward Raymond and then Meredith. " … un-bondables. But … well, you could come to church just once when you're in town." They all laughed. Meredith stood up and hugged him.

"See you in the morning," said Juan, and left to meet Sid at the car. Dinner and weary conversation stretched on in the soft evening breeze of the lagoon until Raymond finally folded his napkin and said, "No one got much sleep last night—except maybe Meredith— so I think we should shut down early."

"With you on that," groaned Tad, pulling his long body out of the chair, weariness curving it. He dropped his own napkin on the table and looked out to the sea. The trade winds blew his longish hair. He pushed back the mane with his hand. "Whew. Well, T.K. you wanted us to have some time to decompress, talk and put feet back on the ground. I don't know there's much more to say or feel after this past twenty-four hours. Except maybe Mission Accomplished." He extended a hand to help Meredith up. She smiled at his chivalry and accepted. "See you in the morning—for breakfast with Sid, I guess." He ambled off the patio and toward his own room.

Raymond put his arm around Meredith and together they walked to their own hut.

"I'd ask you to tell me about the exciting world of Hawaii show business," sighed Raymond, sinking down to the bed and pulling off his sandals. "But I'm not sure I'd be very good company and would probably fall asleep. No disrespect or disinterest intended."

"Don't worry," Meredith assured him. "I'll get you in the morning—and it won't be with show biz stories." She dropped her flowered dress to the floor, turned her head over her bare shoulder and winked at him.

As the sun came up full on the cloistered village of thatched huts, Meredith made good on her promise—with no complaints from Raymond. "The salve that heals," he murmured, snuggled tightly against her.

"I suppose we should get up," she sighed. "Hate to miss breakfast with the holy terror."

"No need to worry," he assured her. "Remember it only seems like mid-morning. We're three hours behind our usual time zone.

"Well, then … silly to waste those hours."

They finally managed to rise, shower and dress and find their way to the patio restaurant before any others had arrived.

"I need to tell you that I passed along to Tad that old black and white photo you found from the 'legendary' Hollywood apartment building—the one showing his mother, Lindy, with my dad."

"The one at a party, with her on his lap?" asked Meredith, clearly uncertain about the wisdom of the gift.

"That one," said Raymond with no hint of question. "It's the only visual he'll ever have of the two of them. It won't mean something as tawdry to him as it means to us."

"How's he doing otherwise?" she probed.

"Oh, he has a good life, Meredith. Loves his work, is respected, likes where he lives and seems to have friends. But he is very focused on his work as a software engineer. Most techies are. But, he's doing fine other than his granddad's death and well … this now."

The tall figure of Tad Oakley appeared on the path heading toward them. "I can't believe how much like you he is," Meredith chuckled, taking a large drink of coffee. "But so young he looks more like your offspring than your brother—and more so than your real son Will does—and certainly more than Riley!"

"She's lucky," Raymond countered, perusing the breakfast menu. "She looks like you and what a gift for her!" Meredith blushed.

"Good morning," Tad said in an enthusiastic greeting. "Amazing what a good night's sleep does!"

"I'll say," Raymond agreed. Meredith concentrated on her menu.

"What do you think we can expect this morning?" the young man asked. "More histrionics? Apologies? Think he'll show?"

"Maybe some of it all," Meredith suggested. The waitress arrived with a sunny "Aloha, Kakahiaka—Good morning." And they ordered food. Before it arrived, Sid did. Juan following discreetly behind.

"Good morning," Raymond quickly spoke up. "Great breakfast menu. Sit." He gestured to the two vacant chairs, ever the polite host. Sid's eyes had soft purple circles beneath the orbs, but his skin color was a healthier pink than Meredith remembered it being the evening before. His hair was combed, and he looked rested. A good cry can do that for you, she thought—some knowledge lurking from her own past.

"Here," she handed her menu to Sid. "Great selections. And local fresh papaya. Absolutely the best."

"Thanks. Sounds good," He uttered as he took the menu from her. Juan signaled the waitress and ordered coffee and a bagel. Three sets of eyes looked at him. He shrugged and raised apologetic brows.

"I don't get bagels very often."

"I have some work to do," Sid suddenly spoke up, mostly studying his coffee cup. "I guess I've been a dickhead. I keep thinking about what a bright little girl Lynnie was. And how innocent and naïve. I can't get the image out of my head of her lying in some sandy grave. How someone killed her. It's haunted me— and I'm confused about how all our lives weren't what we thought."

"No one's ever really is, but none of ours … " Raymond waved a hand indicating the table, "has really resulted in too many setbacks. And we don't know whether Lynnie was happy with her choices up until she died. We know she didn't choose to leave behind a little boy she cherished."

"I don't remember anything but Ed's house and it's many gifts, and the stories about my mother," Tad countered.

"But I'm confused," said a much humbled Sid. "Why tell us at all? Now or any time?" He looked intently at Raymond. "And why so recently—so long after she died? Did anyone need to know this?"

"I did," Tad said. "Like being adopted and thinking you weren't until you realized you were. The truth can be clarifying … "

"Somehow these kinds of secrets always come out," Raymond said. "The truth was a surprise, but important to me, too. Until I was called in to investigate a murder—of an unknown actress who'd been buried for decades—no one had any idea about this whole situation. And, Sid, we both had a blood tie to this young man," he indicated Tad, "which we should have been aware of. Your sister kept her secrets and left the world with them. My dad did too. I needed to know I had a brother."

"So did I." Tad seemed to close the discussion as the food arrived and the waitress set down plates. First bites about to be taken when a booming voice overtook the table.

"Aloha—Meredith!" Coming up the path in his recognizable swagger was Brent Silver, the hunky star of *Honolulu Confidential*. Meredith had spent several hours around him only a couple of days before.

"Brent," she exclaimed, "What a surprise to see you again—so soon. Shouldn't you be on set over on Oahu?"

He laughed heartily. "They gave me the rest of the week off so they could center around Selma," he said referring to his female costar. "My buddy has a fishing boat here and we're going out in a few minutes." He extended his hand to the assembled group at the table, each shaking it perfunctorily.

Sid seemed lightning struck paralyzed as Meredith introduced everyone. Eyes sparkling and voice almost in a gasp, he blurted, "My family watches your show all the time! We're big fans."

Brent's face stretched into a wide toothpaste-commercial smile and said, "I love to meet my fans and welcome to Hawaii." Sid fumbled into his bag and dug out a small snapshot camera.

"Would you mind if I took a picture?" The actor grinned his most theatrical grin and said, "Not at all." Meredith jumped up, snatched the camera, placed the two next to each other with the palm trees and lagoon in the background and snapped off several shots.

"Any of you guys want to go fishing?" Brent asked, turning cordial and sincere. "We've got extra room on the boat. Going after the big guys—marlin—be back by five or six." Tad looked up like a small boy offered an ice cream cone. He didn't need to say anything.

"Go ahead, Tad," Raymond urged. "Take advantage. You and I have surely had all the time and opportunity needed to process about family. But I'm staying here with Meredith—we have some shopping to do." She smiled wickedly.

Sid looked up enviously but stepped back. "I think I'd better go home," he sighed." I have a flight leaving in a little while."

Brent wrote out directions and schedule for Tad, hugged Meredith and bid everyone else goodbye, striding off with his friend toward the lobby. Tad was busily eating his fruit bowl and scattering the eggs around on his plate, eyes remaining wary. The somber subject that had blossomed into animosity and anger for the past two days seemed to have withered. Breakfast finished, Juan stood up and tapped Sid on the shoulder. "Time to ride, partner," he said with a cowboy accent. He looked at Meredith and Raymond. "Dinner tomorrow?" They nodded.

Lowered emotional temperatures eased out of the gathering as Sid picked up his bags preparing to leave. The burly figure, sporting a new baseball cap that said "Aloha" on the brim turned toward the lobby pathway and a fragile sense of relief saw Tad, Raymond and Meredith sneaking furtive glances at one another. Tad suddenly launched himself from his chair and caught up with his uncle.

"Call me, Uncle Sid, if you need to talk," the young man offered, reaching out to touch his uncle's arm. Sid turned and looked at him, eyes tearing up.

"Sorry kid. You had to know her." Then he unexpectedly swiveled toward Meredith and Raymond.

"What a trip! Not exactly the best reason for coming all the way to Hawaii—but all's well huh? Met some new friends and I even got to see a beautiful secret lagoon in Kona—and best of all, I met Brent Silver!"

"Can't wait to tell Sally and the kids about that!"

Kona Village Resort is described by many as an icon of the sunny coast of Hawaii Island, "the Big Island." Built in 1965 around ancient fishponds in a verdant oasis on a lagoon, access was only by boat or private plane. A road was eventually added. Hales, or bungalows, originally featured decor by favorite Hawaiian designer Mary Philpotts, original art by iconic artist Pegge Hopper. No radios, TVs, phones, audible music, or noises—pre-cell phone days. In 2011, the grounds were destroyed by tsunami and were only rebuilt and reopened in 2023. Again, only inaudible cell communication allowed on the grounds, and still the quiet elegance of a special place.

ITO IN THE NIGHT
1997

1997
ITO IN THE NIGHT

Meredith slid quietly out of bed, trying not to waken her sleeping husband, slipped on her robe, and padded, barefoot, down the stairs into the living room. She paused instinctively at the bottom step and looked around the expanse of the living room and adjoining kitchen. Paco, the large grey cat had slipped silently from the second upstairs bedroom—the one where Meredith's four-year-old daughter, Riley, slept. Where the cat usually slept. Golden eyes peering into the dark, the feline scanned the same room as the human. On high alert. They'd both heard the same barely-audible sounds coming from the beach in front of the house. Even the surf was quiet tonight yet uncharacteristic noises seem to carry above it. Meredith crossed the floor to the sliding glass doors onto the veranda and its ocean view, cat trailing in her wake. Both, individually, scrutinized the sand intently. Curiosity was instinctive. She an investigative journalist. He, a cat.

Guardedly, she eased open the sliding door and slipped out onto the deck. Paco squeezed between her feet to the same destination. And they both watched for action on the beach.

The night over the ocean was as calm and clear as they'd ever seen it. A summer star-glistened night, and only small but frothy waves visiting the shore. Nearby, Ito had parked his car on the street and quietly nudged the car door closed, clasping his heartfelt package to his chest. The slightly-built Japanese man was comfortable navigating the well-heeled neighborhood—elegant homes mostly belonging to the celebrated. His Los Angeles "family"—family of long-time colleagues and friends—lived in one of the houses. The one where the woman and the feline were keeping watch on the beach. He cut a slight figure as he meandered the path between the homes, slipped off his shoes, and in his sockless feet trudged through the sand to the waterside. The soft grittiness of the beach felt comforting and familiar.

Ito lived in Venice Beach, some 20 miles south, but to him, the Malibu shore front belonging to Meredith Ogden and husband T.K. Raymond was more like home. He looked up at the three story house, only night safety lights aglow at two in the morning on a weeknight. He smiled at the quiet—rare in the domicile. With the highly charged environment around the residents—her, an international Hollywood columnist and commentator, him a top cop administrator specializing in entertainment industry crimes—the house was often busy, full and noisy. Often with laughter. Sometimes under threat.

But tonight, Ito felt, was his alone. The package he clasped close to his body was heavy. Not so much the weight per se, but the history and value that came with it. It carried the seat of his life since he arrived in the U.S. in 1970.

He had arrived in Los Angeles to attend a UCLA business administration program, fresh from his home in Japan. He became a citizen four years later. His mother and two brothers remained in the small town from which he had immigrated. Throughout his years, they'd never chosen to travel abroad, never to California and surely never to L.A. no matter how compelling his invitations. And with his position now with *News-New York* as the general manager of West Coast On-Air Syndication, he had sent them first class tickets—all unaccepted. At first, he would feel hurt at his family's reluctance to visit and taste his new-found life—so different from their slim and rural beginnings. And so he made up for it by returning to his Japanese roots as often as possible—less so as his life became more complex and integrated, although his ties to his own humble beginnings were never far from his thoughts.

From the time he had arrived in the high energy and ego of the Southern California two decades before, Ito's refuge and home base had been with his Aunt Nico and her family. Like his mother, his aunt was a post war widow. But Nico had come to America in the 1950s, his mother opting to stay in the small village. It was at the urging of Nico that Ito saw a way to explore a world beyond. When he arrived and began classes, he lived with her and his two cousins, a boy and girl about his own age.

He had worked at jobs around the school until he graduated in business administration. By then, his cousins had left the confines of the university and were working full time in insurance and investment. Ito chose to continue education to an MBA. But along the way, he'd been seduced by Hollywood's glitter and was hungry to explore it. He claimed all it took to instill that sense of "wow" was a chance meeting with the *Wonder Woman* star Linda Carter at a fast food restaurant where he worked. Then he glimpsed Burt Reynolds at a hardware store in West L.A. and decided he wanted more of the fantasy.

Through it all, Aunt Nico kept the grounded vigil. When he'd return from a disappointing day at school, a poor grade, a deflated relationship, she talked to him, poured tea, shared her favorite sake and hugged him—uncharacteristic of most of his relatives, even his parents.

When a friend told him of becoming a celebrity houseman through a specialized local employment agency, he hastened to its door. And met Bettina Grant, one of the most widely published Hollywood columnists in the country. He remembered the day he drove his aunt's car to the Bel Air home of the revered journalist. She answered the door, her hair unruly, no makeup, in jeans and a sweatshirt and a cigarette hanging from her fingers.

"This is the place," she said, noncommittally. "Look it over. I've never employed a house person before. You probably know more about it than I do." Ito chose not to contradict her even though he should have. The Grant home was lovely, warm and felt very personal. "The kids have left for college," she explained. "It would be just us and the dog." He saw a panting Shih Tzu looking in through the sliding glass doors to a small pool.

"Here's your quarters," she announced, leading him to a suite off one side of the house, behind the garage. A bedroom with a bed, dresser, couch and small dining table with a compact kitchenette and bathroom. The size and convenience of it amazed him. He'd never had so much space to himself.

"Well?" Bettina Grant demanded. Think it'll work?"

"Don't you want to know more about me?" he asked.

"Do you cook?" she asked. He nodded.

"Can you clean—scrub floors and so on? Serve guests when they're around?" Thinking of his times as a server in restaurants during college, he nodded affirmatively. "Can you drive my Jag?" she pressed on. He thought of the prestige of being behind the wheel of such a grand automobile and nodded a rapid yes.

"What else can you do?" she asked

"I can balance your check book, file your taxes. I have a degree in accounting and am finishing an MBA," he said every so quietly, but with confidence.

The woman's eyes widened in surprise, and she was silent for a moment. "Why are you here? Can't you do better in an accounting firm or big company? With your languages and all … ?"

He smiled shyly and said, "I like to be around show business." And shrugged.

Bettina Grant again fell silent—a rare happenstance Ito was soon to learn. When she spoke, she was somewhat hesitant. "How do you feel about wearing a white houseman's jacket? It's kind of expected, you know."

He smiled. "You'll probably have to shop at a young boy's store. I'm quite small, you may have noticed." It was the end of the interview and the beginning of a new life for Ito.

He smiled at the recollection of his days as the "white jacket" houseman. A role he fulfilled—along with being personal manager and accountant—for Bettina Grant until she was murdered four years later. In the ensuing chaos of finding her killer, keeping the journalism office functioning and focusing on the future, Ito became a member of the Hollywood news reporting team along with the former "legwoman" assistant Meredith Ogden, their secretary Sonia, colleague Cassie O'Connell and ultimately Meredith's lifetime partner special profile detective T.K. Raymond.

As he had shed the white coat, his family of friends grew deep roots. Much of their life pulsated—during daylight hours—in the comely house overlooking the sand stretch where Ito now gazed to sea in the darkness.

He stood at the edge of the surf and took in the stars, chanting quietly to himself, in Japanese, a poem he knew from his own childhood, something his mother had often whispered to him at night. His Aunt Nico had continued the recitation when he'd come home distressed or worn down from the rigors of college in a second language and new customs and routines.

He felt tears brimming, a sense of sad closure. Nico was his lifeline for so long, the one person he returned to visit from his heady days as a New York media junior executive, the one with whom he spent every Sunday afternoon after his long-hungered move back to Los Angeles, now to his current perfectly tailored position. After he had slathered himself in Hollywood and was found the life satisfying, she cheered his successes.

Nico's demise was calm in its slide downward but too quick when it culminated one afternoon. Ito was called to the nursing home, then it was his duty to inform the offspring—neither of whom lived on the west coast. They came for the official ceremonies and the family gathering. But left as quickly as they came. Ito's own mother had already passed on and his own siblings had no connection with the venerable Aunt Nico. He was the major life thread to her.

"It's what they do here," one of his cousins had said, passing over their mother's ashes in a plain copper urn to a perplexed Ito.

He thought it might be a vase. He asked what he should do with it and the ashes—unfamiliar with the American traditions. The cousins shrugged and one said, "Put her—her ashes—where she'd want to spend her days—probably where she spent most cherished times. You, probably more than any of us, would know." Ito thought about the kitchen, but her house was long sold. So, he took the urn to a place that he, himself, most valued. A wonderful place to share with her.

He wrestled the carton to the ground, as he removed the delicate urn. Opening it, he suddenly felt overwhelmed—by the moment, the night, the memories. Then he started to sing softly, surprising even himself, but was startled as a soft firm hand gently rested on his shoulder. He turned around to see his friend, a breeze-tousled Meredith Ogden in her bathrobe.

"It's okay, Ito. Please sing your song," her quiet voice urged.

He sang—faintly, almost whispering the words, "I say a little prayer for you," lyrics from the Dionne Warwick song of the 1960s—his aunt's favorite song. "She liked to sing that," he murmured as he gingerly allowed the ashes to flow into the surf. "She believed it—it made her smile. When she sang it, even I knew everything was okay." Meredith's arm slipped gently around both his shoulders and hugged the small man. She mouthed the lyrics along with him.

Paco the cat, watching from the deck, turned, loped into the kitchen, levitating to the top of the refrigerator—his years-long observation home. Knowing that everything really was okay.

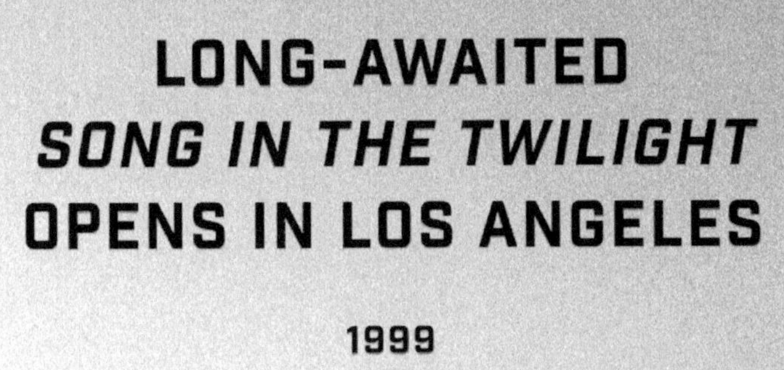

LONG-AWAITED
SONG IN THE TWILIGHT
OPENS IN LOS ANGELES

1999

1999
LONG-WAITED
SONG IN THE TWILIGHT
OPENS IN LOS ANGELES

"Your movie is impressive," said the journalist interviewing a newly minted female producer/director—an anomaly in 1999 filmmaking circles. Her soon to be released film, *Song in the Twilight*, keyed off the female nurses who served in the Vietnam War.

Years after the war, the journalist and filmmaker lounged at a Formica table on the open-air deck of a beach-side grill on the northern edge of Santa Monica and talked about the project. An unusually warm November day, a slight breeze ruffled the canvas overhang above the patio. After lunch and before happy hour, the two were the sole customers inhabiting the popular watering spot .

"About 7,000 American nurses were in the war zone," explained the wiry, brunette producer, her fine facial features unpainted with celebrity decorum and framed in large round black glasses. Mid-thirties, every ounce of her persona seemed strung like a tightly tuned violin, alert, aware, and total present—ready for the moment. "And the stories never end. I interviewed—spent a lot of time with two dozen of them. I felt … humbled. Totally abashed by their stories. So many. So … unbelievable. It became both a privilege and a huge responsibility to be allowed to bring those stories to film—to light. We heard so little about them amid all the rhetoric about the Vietnam War."

Journalist Meredith Ogden appreciated the stance, fell into sync with writer-producer-director Veronica Nesbitt's seriously focused conversation, and unfettered self. No frivolous gestures, no distracting California trendy dialogue, no flirtatious wardrobe additions—or gestures. Just plain black trousers, black turtleneck sweater and simple gold stud earrings. And earnest eyes, dedicated intent.

"I haven't asked the obvious," Meredith explained. "Isn't it a little out-of-the-ordinary for a woman to be telling Vietnam War stories—even if they involve female service individuals? Isn't it a bit heroic on your part to undertake this type of story?"

Veronica chuckled. "I know you had to ask that question—because that's what's on the tongue of most of our filmland colleagues. And yes, I have been asked that many, many times. Most are surprised I had enough of an answer to get past the studio decision-makers and get the funding to do this movie.

"How'd I do it? I had great stories and a great script—but the timing is right. We need to hear these stories. I'm not down-playing the horrific or heroic stories our vets tell about the actual combat and overall hell of experiences in Vietnam. But these women were part of it and their stories need to be told—for everyone, but especially for young women, old women, any women. There are role models and female heroines today. Their stories are important.

"Whew!" she suddenly gasped. "Soap box again. Too much information?"

Meredith laughed. "Preaching to the choir," she answered. "But a sermon I'm exhilarated to listen to. What was the hardest part of making the film?"

"Convincing the mostly-male technical and service community to take this all seriously."

"Elaborate, please," goaded Meredith.

"Everything from makeup people trying to tart up the faces of the actresses playing the nurses to camera shots set to beautify those faces and make really down-and-dirty scenes look too pretty. The male actors wanting to buff up their own roles or lines. Business as usual," she said simply. "And that says nothing about the job of selling the project to ninety-nine percent male studio heads. It was a female casting director at Limelight who forced the hand of the CEO—because he trusted her and was willing to take the risk—to keep her at the studio. That's how dedicated she was to the project. I owe her big time. Obviously, she's cast the movie."

"And brilliantly," Meredith added, noting the stellar and yet unconventional cast filling out the roles. "How did it feel to you to be making a break-through story on film? One you seem to feel totally dedicated to?"

As Veronica thought intently about the questions and answered with total candor, Meredith felt a kindship with the producer, feeling a little like a kindergartener who'd just met the first classmate who resonated with herself.

"When you interviewed the nurses, what was it like? It's been a long time since the war. How were they?"

"You're asking two questions. What was it like? For me. Humbling, sometimes amusing, sometimes distant, always with stories, reminisces. One married one of her patients. Another still keeps in touch with the kids of a wounded soldier. They all remembered stories of the people—friendly and not—with whom they interacted."

"How were they? 'How' is important. Introspective. Sad. Loyal to the effort they put in. Proud of their nurses group. Anxious—about how their words might be taken, what their families would think of them. Excited that someone cared and that their stories would be told."

"We hear and see so many stories of the anguish, atrocities—on all sides—and the traumatic post-war hangover from American military. We hear little about the women," Meredith probed, focusing closely on Veronica's comments. "Is that just the usual write-off as 'War is a man's world?' Were the females who served treated poorly … ?"

Veronica waved off the question. "All of the above, Meredith.

Think about it. There were well over three million Americans who served in Southeast Asia. And only about seven-thousand-five-hundred U.S. women. Of those, a huge majority were nurses. And think of the slice of the action they saw. Not the part we most often see because their work and the outcomes weren't the easiest to talk about—or show if you are thinking of movies or film."

Taking down Veronica's comments Meredith held firm on great accuracy and care. Not all discussions required so much. All the studio publicity information—biography, previous film credits of Veronica Nesbitt—first as an actress, then a writer and then precedent-setting producer and director, plus background on the film—was already in Meredith's bag.

"So, what, for you, was the most eye-opening thing about either the interviewing and writing of the story, or making of the film?" the journalist pressed onward.

"Always how little I know about history. After extensive research, all the interviews and discussions," Veronica shrugged," I always feel like I need to know more, include more, tell more stories."

The discussion went on into the late afternoon. The Sea Shack was empty of customers, but staff hustled around preparing for the happy hour and dinner crowd.

"My film may turn heads and be a surprising subject, but I'm not really the break-through here. Think about Penny Marshall," Veronica stated with reverence. "First woman director with a film—*Big*—to make more than 100 million dollars in the U.S. *Awakenings* got an Oscar nomination. *A League of Their Own* … on and on. But there were many other women directors. Ida Lupino, Jane Campion, long time ago. Today's new entries: Kimberly Pierce, Sophia Coppola. Keep your eye out—there'll be many others coming forward." The two women mused on about the female directors since Leni Riefenstahl—Hitler's filmmaker.

"So, tell me about yourself," Veronica surprisingly veered away from the typical interview patter.

Taken aback a little, Meredith screwed up her face and asked,

"How much do you want to know?" They both laughed. "It's gonna be pretty mundane and boring," the journalist shrugged.

"Dish," the producer intoned, using a typical Hollywood gossip term for "tell all." She beckoned with both hands, urging more information.

"Not much," Meredith answered slightly. "Umm … went to journalism school, came to Hollywood, worked in TV publicity for a while, got a job as a 'legwoman' or assistant with Bettina Grant and just stayed on after she died, making the most of the exciting world she had created. Married to a police detective, a seven-year-old daughter, and live at the beach."

"Tsk-tsk," said Veronica. "Are all hard-hitting journalists so self-effacing?"

"They'd better be," Meredith shrugged. "It's way too easy to think you're the center of it all and with Hollywood journalism now a centrifugal force on TV, self-aggrandizement is actually de rigueur but any journalist should be the observer or even translator but never the center of the conversation." Both women laughed.

"Tell that to the hot lady on *Tonight's Show Biz,*" Veronica sniffed derisively. "After she adjusts her clingy leotards, smiles through the thick theatrical make-up that hasn't dripped even once, as she comes off the exercise machine in those publicity articles. But I ask about you," she continued, "because I'm sincerely fascinated by your career. Work-a-day writer, legwoman, correspondent, bureau manager, top line commentary columnist, TV talk show face. Wife, mother … Don't laugh. I always vet the reporters who interview me. You're no reporter. You're a serious journalist and industry observer/commentator. And you've been a key player in many entertainment industry crime-related stories and situations."

Meredith wagged her head dismissively. "Stories for another day, Veronica. Right now, it's time to be on my way northward to home." The two picked up their afternoon's debris from the table and dropped on in the adjacent trash can, packed up their own belongings and made their way toward the door.

"I'm bringing one of the actual nurses to be with me on the show on Thursday," Veronica said, a question mark at the end of the sentence. "Okay?"

"Great. Added color. Thanks for being my guest," Meredith responded then detoured into the ladies' room. She hosted a weekly one hour Hollywood news segment on the L.A. based *Morning Coffee Show,* a segment fed through syndication to local stations around the country. The show's producer was her long-time colleague, Cassie O'Connell.

As Veronica moved toward the restaurant doorway she called out, "At least write some of your own stories." Meredith waved, answered back, "Thanks—see you at eight a.m. in the studio, Thursday."

Leaving the restroom a few minutes later, the earlier afternoon happy hour crowd was beginning to inhabit the bar section of the comfortable local Sea Shack grill. Meredith scoured her deep shoulder bag as she walked toward the exit, digging for her mobile phone. She looked up and into the row of customers at the scarred wooden bar and saw a familiar face. She froze, instinct reminding her he was important, but she had to search deep in her memory to remind herself why. He turned just enough for her to see more of the countenance, and she knew right way.

Screwing up her courage, she approached the guy—middle aged, sandy hair cut efficiently, a blue polo shirt and chinos, thick build. "Excuse me," she moved into the space next to the stool where he sat. "Duck, isn't it?" The sun-hued weathered face turned and gazed upon her. The shocked flash in his eyes told her he recognized her—maybe not specifically but as someone he didn't want to see.

"Duck," she repeated. "I'm Meredith. You rescued me from being stranded on one of the military ghost ships in Suisan Bay up in San Francisco Bay—oh, six-seven years ago." She caught the recognition in his face, but he shook his head.

"Sorry, who? When?" he stammered, sounding almost rehearsed.

"In Suisan Bay. You snatched me off a ship where I'd been left behind and dropped me in the marina a ways away. You were delivering something that day." She was already framing the conversation with detail because she recalled how hard the Northern California authorities—Coast Guard, Police—as well at Raymond and his FBI friends had searched for the guy.

Looking directly at her, he answered, "I'm sorry I think you have the wrong person." She noted the small tattoo on the side of his neck—the one she'd originally seen so many years ago and had hoped it would help find him.

"Oh, I'm sure it was you. I tried to find you to thank you with some kind of a reward later but … well … the Loma Prieta Earthquake and all. The Coast Guard found your boat but we never found you. I'm so glad you didn't drown. Are you living here now?"

He abruptly looked at his watch and rose from the stool "Sorry, I have an appointment, gotta go. Not me, lady." She watched him move briskly to the door, out and into the parking lot. She watched him find a dark blue SUV, unlock it and in record time, drive off onto the highway. She jotted down the license number and make of the vehicle just in case, then went to her own car.

Anxious to call T.K. Raymond about the discovery of the infamous "Duck," Meredith came through her own kitchen door with a "whoosh" and headed for her office. All manner of law enforcement had searched for the mysterious boatman who'd plucked Meredith from the shipboard film location on which she'd been accidentally left behind. A half dozen years had passed and now he'd shown up at the beachside bar ten minutes from the house.

"Missus Meredith, Missus Meredith … " Lupe the house helper called out in haste—more in demand. Bringing the journalist to an immediate halt, turning to see the round grey-haired figure standing in the hallway, hands on hips.

"What?" she snapped.

"A lady named Maribelle Davis called. Very important, she said. Must talk with you immediately." Meredith's heart sank. She could not dismiss Maribelle—the woman had saved Riley from abduction three years before. By sitting on the would-be abductor with her 300 pound figure and fearless courage. Meredith felt herself almost dizzy with the competing mandates.

She chose Maribelle, with a sigh, and placed the call. "Oh gawd, thank goodness," spewed the large woman, the mother of a classmate of Riley's from the first day of kindergarten. "Selma was supposed to sing *I'll be Home for Christmas*—our closing and most transcendent song in the kids' school holiday concert next week. The kids have been practicing the harmony all month long. But Selma's mother is ill and she has to leave town. We don't have another parent with the voice, and I hoped—well maybe—you could talk one of your … " she cleared her throat and continued meekly, "contacts, show biz friends … to sub … please." Mirabelle's voice had dropped to a near-whisper in full beseeching mode.

Feeling her constitution flagging, Meredith rolled her eyes and eked out, "Let me see what I can do, Maribelle. I can't promise. It's a very busy time of the year … "

"Maybe someone who lives close by?" peeped Maribelle.

"I'll call you back." Meredith hung up and quickly punched in Raymond's number on her phone. "I found Duck," she crowed as he picked up.

"What?" he fumbled.

"Duck—the guy who took me off the ship—the Ghost Ship in San Francisco Bay—the guy you've all looked for. Thought maybe he drowned in the Earthquake."

"Oh, yeah," Raymond said. "Duck." Meredith gave him the license number from the SUV, its description and an update on that of the man himself.

"I have to go," she sighed. "I have to find a singer for Maribelle—for the kids holiday concert."

"Oh. Damn. I almost forgot about that."

"Come on now. It can't be as bad as one of the studio or network parties," she teased.

"No, I guess you're right. No tuxedos. See you in a little while."

They disconnected as their seven year old daughter bounded down the stairs from her room, brandishing some flyleaf pages and yelling, "Mom, mom—look at the pretty dresses we're going to wear in the Christmas concert!"

Excited, involvement on the elementary school level continued for a while interspersed with calls to several school parents who sing. And a couple of good friends who might be willing to sing in a kids' gathering, then a check of work and office calls before Raymond came through the door, dizzy with news of his own.

"I need to talk about something with you. Something serious." Meredith sat up, alert, and gazed at him.

"Bill Perkins from Sterner Elsworth came to see me about two months ago. I mentioned it then. You know them, right? Big creative management group? Handles the business of a large roster of high profile clients—actors, directors, musicians?" Meredith nodded in recollection.

"Elsworth took me to lunch today—a follow-up to a very brief conversation back then. That was after my department had to step in to diffuse a very hyper-electric conflict between their client, a musician, and a union. Apparently, the type of conflict that the firm sees a lot. Also the kind of situation I've spent most of my life resolving. Along with celebrities who've beat up their family members, shot someone, or run over someone." Meredith let out a titter-type chuckle.

"Elsworth was already slathering me with praise and accolades. You also know that since Bernie left, our unit has not been given a lot of love from P.D. Headquarters. Rumors that we'll be moving back to downtown L.A., that we'll be dissected—reassigned and … the group pretty much dissolved."

"Well, Bernie liked to have a desk here in the west side of town—and closer to his home out here. Your team gave him that opportunity."

"I could comfortably resign. I have the years and full pension. But … "

"It's not where you're at yet," Meredith finished the thought.

"With my law license as well as a new P.I. license and experience, Elsworth is offering me a nice berth. Special Legal Liaison, emphasis in working with law enforcement when a client gets into one of those law-challenging situations and needs a good negotiator—everything from troublesome DUIs to homicides. Westwood offices close by, flexible schedule, work from home when needed, very nice money. And, I'll still have my pension."

"Really big change," she declared , holding her breath so as not to disrupt his train of thought or seem in any way negative. "Are you up for it?"

Raymond shrugged. "I'm not up for redeveloping the whole landscape at work—again, having to reestablish relationships and constant rationalizing the worth of our unit. It doesn't matter that we've proven the value so often. The 'new' PD is about budgets and saving money. Ted Klingsman in my unit—the real estate investigator—seems to want a leadership role. I'm thinking it's time to let him have it. Mine. And he can fight the new wave of bureaucracy."

"Isn't it kind of life as usual over the many years you've been in that 'high profile' investigator role?"

"But we always had our champion in Bernie. We haven't one now. And I don't want to have to be it. Too old, I guess."

Meredith looked at him and smirked. "I'm behind whatever you want to do, Raymond. It's your turn to take a risk. God knows how often I've done it. Just let me know what I can do. It'll be an adjustment for us all."

He smiled at her and she could see the slight apprehension in his eyes. Something she rarely saw. But she knew it was a new, unknown path. They would make it work.

"When?" she asked.

"Ninety days," he grimaced. She, too, felt a grimace but remembered how often they'd undertaken new roadways and how satisfying they'd always turned out to be.

• • •

On Thursday, on the *Morning Coffee Show* on which Meredith appeared weekly, Veronica and her nurse guest provided robust discussion and entertainment. The filmmaker had previously invited both Meredith and the show's producer—Meredith's long-time friend and former colleague—Cassie O'Connell to join her for lunch at a nearby bistro. Always good for a post-show break, they agreed. After Meredith sloshed off the camera make-up and put on comfortable work clothes, and Veronica bid the nurse guest adieu with profound thanks, they joined Cassie, hoofing quickly to the restaurant.

A man and woman were seated at the table where the hostess directed them. The two sat languidly, well-dressed in California casual, comfortable and confident. Both Meredith and Cassie became slightly cautious when they first arrived, but Veronica quickly dissuaded them from concern. "Meet the Zellmans," she said introducing the strangers. "Debra and Soras. They've been my executive producers on three different project including *Song in the Twilight*. Handshakes and smiles ensued as the three women took their seats.

"I invited you both here for a great lunch—it's my favorite place," Veronica explained. "But I wanted you to meet these two good friends. And talk with us about something I think would be interesting for us all." Cassie and Meredith glanced at one another. They'd been through years of misadventures, intended scams, bad taste escapades, and winning exploits as well. Their immediate and traditional take on most proposals was one of doubt, hesitancy.

"But let's eat, first," interjected Veronica. The forthrightness was only matched by the intent focused on her face. The air lightened, lunch was ordered and idle conversation was in progress when Meredith's mobile phone rang. She apologized for neglecting to turn it off and glanced at it. She excused herself for a moment and hurried out into the entrance.

"Mirabelle. I'm in a meeting. What's happening?"

"Just to say thanks. Thanks to you, Nella Jarvis has agreed to sing the finale. So perfect—a sixth-grader's mother who's a professional who sings with the back-ups on Idol."

"Great," sighed Meredith. "So, we're good. You're ready to go?"

"Yep—just a huge thank you. See you in a couple of weeks at the kids' concert!" An immediate whoosh of relief passed over Meredith as one of those tiny little tasks had been accomplished, no longer occupying space and time in her head. Raymond's scoff about no tuxedo necessary at the concert rang in her memory. She returned to the group at the table, feeling anxiously curious about the topic that was to come.

"Sorry," she said, sliding into her dining chair. A lively conversation was underway, her absence barely noticed.

"We were talking about the drama, pathos, craziness and seriousness of the stories you've covered over the years," Cassie spoke up. Meredith shrugged self-consciously, taking a distracting sip from the iced tea glass recently refilled. A few drops dribbled from the over-filled glass. She busied herself blotting up the wetness from the table.

"Here's what I want to talk about," Veronica broke through the distractions. She reached into her case and extracted a handful of pages, then passed them out to each of the table partners. "Deb and Soras have worked with me for a long time and they know about what I'm suggesting, actually helped define it." Meredith and Cassie felt the sisterhood pull, unseen or known by anyone other than themselves, developed over many shared experiences with unknown outcomes.

"I've watched your stories, Meredith. Over many years. Anyone in the movie or TV industry had no choice. You're that pervasive. But also known a lot of your colleagues and compatriots and they've talked a lot about the intricacies and mysteries of those stories. Bob Milas, head of programming for CBA, talked to me recently about what the network would like to develop as a series with a woman in the key role but with the opportunity for not only deep, dark crime, but broad segments in different situations, locations and a character who is both heroic and ordinary. But stoic and focused—a female stalwart superstar."

Meredith felt her face cloud and wrinkle in confusion but remained silent.

"If you read the pages I've handed you," Veronica continued, "you'll see I've outlined a treatment for a pilot that features a TV series character based on your adventures."

Meredith was still shaking her head subtly, in a continued state of disbelief and confusion. Cassie folded her hands in her lap and stared down at the placemat.

"Well, I wouldn't define my work over these years as a series of adventures," Meredith proffered. "It's just … well … my work. What a journalist does when she gets up in the morning, goes to her desk or keyboard or phone—or wherever the story is—digs out that story and tells it."

"But those stories are a fascinating backbone—a rich skeleton of someone's—your—daily professional life. Colorful and sometimes thought-provoking, sometime titillating … " the filmmaker searched for more words. "Always interesting."

'I've never seen myself as that kind of 'character,'" Meredith stammered.

"And the stories are so often about known celebrities and stars, the legal ramifications would be horrendous," mothered Cassie.

"This would be fictional," Deb Zellman spoke up. "Each episode or combination of episodes would follow the reporter through the steps to unlock a story, track down a source, fend off perpetrators. Making the gossip columnist the center point, the key focus with the activity swirling around her."

Meredith eyes grew wide before she spoke up. "I haven't covered 'gossip' for ten years, Deb. If that's the direction, you need the pretty lady from *Tonight's Show Biz,* and I imagine her network would love to see that. I don't think you would want a show about the ins and outs of politics with a political gossip columnist as your role model … ”

"Or maybe you would … " interjected Cassie with a question in the statement.

"My very bad choice of words," Deb jumped in, her throaty voice rushing the words. "We want a serious heroine, not a cheesy funny or silly character. That's why Veronica has been watching you."

Meredith was quiet and stared at the papers in front of her but not really focusing on them. The whole idea was so foreign, so unexpected she couldn't even evaluate her own thoughts.

"Why don't we take some time to look over the treatments you've given us," said Cassie. "And I wonder what I'm doing here. I produce a daily morning talk show. My days as an entertainment chronicler were long ago and brief."

"We need a line producer," said Deb. "Someone who knows the TV production and understands the story lines and the character—very well." Cassie felt her own eyebrows raising.

"Someone to make the trains run on time," snicked Soras, the sole male at the table. "We'd be the executive producers—along with Meredith and Veronica—who would be named the creators as well. Veronica would do the storylines with Meredith—and probably you, too, Cassie—and direct the episodes."

Sitting tall, silent and neutral, Meredith tried to process the proposal, wondering if it was real or some kind of a grift. But Veronica had impeccable credits, as did the Zellmans. She realized she would have to use her considerable industry contacts to check out the veracity of this thing before she ever considered it.

"Let me show the list of actors we're considering for the leads—three of them." The list was impressive in its thoughtfulness as well as star power. Some names were only known for their high quality work instead of their celebritydom.

"You've talked to these people already?" Meredith asked.

All three producers nodded. "All but one were enthused about it." Both Meredith and Cassie wondered which one nixed the idea, why, and what, exactly "enthused" meant.

The lunch broke up with Meredith and Cassie agreeing to take a few days to examine the project and offer their thoughts. They agreed to talk with no other media personality or reporter about it, but that didn't mean they couldn't investigate the individuals for their known reputation and modes of operation.

"This is really unnerving," Meredith said to Cassie as they walked back to the studio and their cars.

"Don't let's look a gift horse in the mouth, Meredith," the tall, bubbling brunette-turned-silver-haired producer murmured. "Let's each take two days and do the diligence with our own contacts about these folks. We both have our own set of experts and deep throats in the industry. How about we reconvene over the week-end. Russ'll be in town, and we could get the gang together for dinner." Russ Talbot was Meredith's decades-long boss at two different media networks, Cassie's as well—and for the past few years, Cassie's main man.

Meredith agreed, her mind deeply engaged in the mystery put on the table before them. Once home and pushing through the garage door into the kitchen she knew she had some heavy discussion ahead with Raymond once the house was still again. The chaotic bustle of their household took over the moment she entered. And didn't hush until late into the evening when seven-year-old Riley, Lupe and the cat were curled up into slumberland in their own bed chambers.

"Mirabelle isn't going to let up," muttered Meredith as she came into the living room and flung herself into the largest, most comfortable chair in the room. "First it was the singer. Now it's a costumer. She wants the girls to have special angel dresses."

"This is our elementary school, right? Not the Palladium?" Raymond snarked.

"Yes, but Mirabelle doesn't do anything half-way. And the

parents assigned her to be the holiday concert producer. She thinks I'm in direct control of all things showbusiness—singers, costumes."

"Say 'no'?"

"I still see her pushing that dude to the ground all those years ago and sitting on him—all 300 pounds of her—as he tried to kidnap Riley. I'll always feel that I owe her." Raymond laughed, but knowingly about the episode.

"And," Meredith sighed. "Riley has decided—'absolutely'—that she's going to be an astronaut! She already had researched what she'd have to study and where and what she needed to do NOW. Raymond, it's cast in concrete: we're never going to be able to retire."

"Over achiever," he smirked. "Like her mother," he added with some irony.

"And her dad," Meredith countered, as Raymond slipped into the kitchen to find a bottle of particularly mellow brandy, two appropriate snifters and poured some of the golden liquid for them both. He handed her a glass.

She looked at his face, serious but not too, and his dedicated focus on whatever conversation was to come next. She accepted the snifter, took a grateful sip and looked up at him, questions in her eyes.

"What?"

"Duck," he answered simply. She tilted her head, squinted, puzzled. "We've closed the book."

"Why? He's resurfaced and right here locally."

Raymond smiled at her contritely. "I'm sorry. Quite a while ago I got a report from my good friend in the Coast Guard. The one who kick-started one of the searches for you. After all the collaborative consternation with the local sheriff, PD and even a couple of FBI wonks at the time, the search for you and the subsequent search for 'Duck' got a lot of attention. Almost too much."

Meredith shook her head in confusion. "What does that mean?"

The quest to find the guy in Suisan Bay delivering packages and being both baffling in what seemed illegal activity—and yes, kind to you—ended up in the heart and soul of the ATF center in the San Francisco area. Duck," he cleared his throat, "is an undercover agent. Being nice to you almost blew his gig. The earthquake was a blessing. Gave his group an excuse for him to disappear."

Meredith slunk back into the sofa and blew out a gasp. "No wonder he wasn't even acknowledging me today. 'Course he probably wouldn't have in any case, but … "

"Nothing. Forget you ever saw him and remember him as a kindly recreational boat guy who helped you escape from that big bad ghostly ship seven or so years ago." Raymond took a hearty sip of his brandy. He looked at her for agreement.

"'Kay," she nodded and helped herself to another short pour of the golden balm, feeling slightly left out and a little deflated all this time after the intense drama that had taken place in Suisan Bay. "You might have told me," she quietly retorted.

"I know," he agreed humbly.

But today's topic on her mind was looming large, edging its way into her mind and she pushed the Duck episode aside in order to get it on the table.

"Know anything about astrology?" she asked, sipping her brandy. Raymond shook his head. "Only what I read in the paper each morning in anticipation of my day." He grinned.

"Well, the stars must be aligning—or not. Change is a-comin'," she said flatly. "Or is at least flirting with us a lot these days." Experience kept Raymond sitting stoically without comment. She told him of the encounter with Veronica and the Zellmans. Their proposal, how confounded and conflicted she was over it.

After a few moments, the detective spoke up—cautiously. "What scares you?" he asked. She ran a finger around the rim of the glass and thought about it.

"Everything."

"Start with the first thing," he gently pushed.

"Something that seems promising and maybe is, but is so early and in the 'playing around' stages it overtakes everything and goes nowhere. Becomes humiliating."

"What else?" he asked settling back into the sofa and regarding her carefully.

"Losing credibility over that 'nothing' if it gets blown out of proportion."

"But is there maybe 'something' there?"

"That's the work I have to do over the next week. Cassie and I."

"I can help. My sources are kind of off the beaten path, but definitely in the heartbeat category of some of the studios and power centers." She nodded.

"Russ will be in town this weekend. Cassie and I thought we could have a strategy session with you and him and … "

"Alan," said Raymond with certainty.

"His knees might be weak, but his mind is still sharp," Meredith added. "Maybe he can lend some perspective." She was also already wondering if Alan might be the one to sort out the benefit from the hype and negotiate something that would actually be good for her and Cassie.

Raymond knew that would be on her mind.

✫ ✫ ✫

Sunday morning Raymond, Meredith, Cassie, Russ were piled into Raymond's SUV and arrived at the Sunshine Movie-TV-Music Farm, retirement home to many of Hollywood's luminaries. Alan lived in a two-bedroom apartment there, now alone after his partner of decades, "Potty" Parker Osborn, was living separately in an Alzheimer unit. Alan opened the door to Meredith, pulling on a thick woolen jacket over his camel-colored sweater vest. At ninety, his once-stately figure bent slightly, and he bore only scant clumps of white hair on his head, but Alan Jaymar still held court with his quixotic eyes.

The group motored to the long-lived Calabasas watering hole, the Sagebrush Cantina, settled into an outdoor table under the eaves, and ordered chips and salsa to start.

"I looked at your proposal," Alan spoke up after catch-up chatter wore itself down. "I'd be interested in what Russ has to say. He's a little closer to the here and now on media." Russ wagged his head and deferred. "You first, Alan. You have the fresh but well-honed eyes."

Alan took the proposal step by step, unraveling, bolstering, complimenting, uncoupling. His summary, "The players are strong. Zellmans have been very careful and competent. No bad marks. A few false starts but the wisdom to pull the plug before everything got out of hand. They've never bankrupted any of their money people," he chuckled. "And they've had some very successful long running series. Veronica—the 'it' girl at the moment. Three hot hits with a tough new movie coming out. Her TV track record is unknown—you could do good things for one another."

"The concept, characters and story line. As one of my friends, a program retired exec with one of the studios said, 'valid and promising as most. Will all depend on the scripts, the actors and the director." He paused a moment for a drink of the golden bubbly brew placed before him.

"Glad I'm not driving," he laughed heartily. "As if I could—but, Merri, Cassie—you need a good, wise attorney. Someone who knows his way around this stuff. At least, I can help with that."

Then Raymond spoke up, knowing his words might be more directed and succinct than waiting for Meredith to say her mind more politely. "I think Meredith worries that the series work will overshadow and even entirely smother her newspaper and magazine presence. Not so much for the syndicate and her editors, but with her own attention span. And if the series is not successful, then all the build-up and steeple-building will have been for nothing and only debris would be left of her current much loved work." He looked at Meredith in question. "Did I get that right? She smiled and nodded.

"I have the same issues," said Cassie, breaking a large crisp tortilla chip in half. "I'm getting a little long-in-the-tooth to make risky career changes, especially without the benefit of a great retirement fund and all. And, I like doing my morning show and also it's doing well."

Russ Talbot readjusted his solid body in the heavy wooded restaurant chair and spoke up. "I do have a few things to add," he said. "First, what I know of the folks involved is fine. They're not the very top line TV creators but they're respected and successful. Maybe that's why they're not top of the line. I think you have to have taken a huge risk and fail then come back to be a headliner," he snuffed out a chuckle. Ran a hand through his silver hair.

"But here's another bit of light to shed on the situation. I was going to wait a while to talk about this, but … well, it seems appropriate now. *News-New York* is selling off its syndicated division. Just in the past week, sale completed. It'll take about six months to take effect but," he swallowed and paused.

"*News-New York* wants to syndicate only its own writers, reporters, etc. No outside creative such as yourself, Meredith. The new owners of the broadcast services are British and moving all U.S. broadcast entities to New York. That affects you, Cassie, and with regard to your weekly Hollywood spot, you too Meredith." The controlled gasps and rapid responses, and questions, seemed to buzz around the table like honeybees to a sunflower.

"Can they do that without some kind of pay off?" Cassie demanded.

Russ muttered affirmation. "We're working on something, but it'll be a battle and never what it should be. You'll not have any problem moving elsewhere, Meredith. I've had conversations with the three big news companies in the main cities that already carry your columns. All three now syndicate their own writers. I think we can move you over to one of them—the one that has the best syndicated circulation and most generous funding. IF you want to do that.

"Cassie—your best available option is to move to New York to stay with the show, but I can't promise it'll be the same show or experience you have now. And you'll have different bosses. We can talk more about it."

Alan seemed troubled. Raymond stunned. Meredith angry. Cassie deflated.

"You, Russ? What does this mean for you?" Cassie asked, clearly personally invested in the answer.

The stolid media executive could only shrug. "I'm reviewing my assets and resources so I can logically look at my options. But folks, I'm sixty-eight years old. The only downside to retirement for me is how to fill my days. I've been thinking about a move full-time to the West Coast. I can pretty much play golf year-round." No one responded, all suddenly carried into the imaginings taking place in their own minds. Russ and Cassie had been together as a couple for half a decade and worked together for years before that.

Meredith started to calculate Cassie's age, remembering that the curly-haired silver-streaked brunette had been Bettina Grant's legwoman for eight years before Meredith took over the post when Cassie moved on. That put Cassie in her late fifties. Meredith never thought of the age difference between them, always considered her simply as a colleague and friend.

Alan broke the pensive lull by offering to meet with the Zellmans and Veronica with Meredith and Cassie to further unpack the proposal in real terms. All things considered, the potential for the series seemed even more interesting after Russ's announcement. "Well," mused octogenarian Alan, "lots of moving parts in search of a system here." He looked around at the assembled group at the scarred table. "And, as they say, it's not over until the fat lady sings!"

A youthful patron at the next table full of energetic and noisy twenty-somethings, shot Alan an angry glance accented by an audible sigh. "Not politically correct to denigrate a woman's size," murmured Cassie.

"Should I explain it's a traditional saying based on operatic legacy that the opera's not over until the always-large soprano sings the final notes?" asked Alan.

"No," came a bevy of responses from around the table.

"And anyway," Raymond added quietly, "the non-high-culture story behind the saying comes from the days when commerce ships were steam powered, the large boiler named 'the fat lady.' When the pressure built up and was ready for travel, a whistle sounded letting the shore-side sailors know it was time to board. Ergo—'The fat lady sings … '" Eyes rolled in faces around the table.

Food was served—enchiladas, carne asada and other succulent Mexican dishes with high-heat spice and more pitchers of cerveza. Raymond and Meredith's group left as a bluegrass band came to the small stage and the afternoon's music began. A long-haired, banjo-playing man stepped up and belted out the first notes. And nary a fat woman sang.

On the ride back to the Sunshine Farm to drop off Alan, Raymond revealed his own coming career change. The car-full seemed again stunned, then abuzz with questions.

"T.K., you sound hesitant," Alan commented.

"I don't know how to be anything else," said Raymond. "I'm leaving the police department because I've loved the role I played in the arena—special profile—since I stepped into it and helped build it. But it's about to disappear now," he paused for a moment, then added, "think about how a senior top tennis player must feel when the game is changed into badminton. Rather not do it than always be disappointed and frustrated."

By the time Meredith and Raymond picked up Riley from Gloria Masner's house, chatted briefly with the brunette lawyer and her affable husband, and returned home with their seven-year-old, noisy with stories of her day, the couple were spent. From the conversation heavy with province and prospects to potential, promise and possibility.

"All of us, what is this?" murmured Raymond, helping Meredith put dishes away after dinner. "Fate taking aim at the tried and true, forcing new avenues for everyone. Is this the normal vestige of older age? Russ, Cassie, me, you?"

Meredith simply chuckled. "I've had to detour and adapt most of my career," she said simply. "You've been alongside most of it. It's just another side road to some other main artery. You, however," she put a hand on his cheek, "Are the epitome of mastering the fairway, staying the course. Look at this as just another set of links to be played. You have the skills and the tools, even the vocabulary—just finding a new wardrobe and clubhouse." He shook his head.

"And besides," she intoned, "Maribelle needs me to pick up some tutus for her from some defunct dance school—costumes for the school festivities. Riley says she's going to do hip hop, but I cannot imagine Mirabelle letting anyone cut loose like that in HER production. She's all … " Meredith waved her hands, "angels and twinkling stars."

Raymond shook his head. "When is this extravaganza?"

"Next weekend."

The week in between was filled with adamant purpose for everyone. Meredith, Cassie, Alan and an attorney-friends of his met with the TV producers. Veronica met Alan with much surprise. Meredith suspected that she assumed the women would be making their own decision from their own assessment of the situation. The Zellmans welcomed Alan with great warmth. They knew of his background and reputation, were surprised he'd come out of retirement to oversee the options put forth.

By weekend, an agreement had been executed, a very loose outline of a plotline sketched for a TV series featuring a hard core reporter covering Hollywood toughest stories, and all the logistics hammered out. Final approvals and anointment from the network executives was pending but there seemed to be no obvious obstacles.

Other arrangements were under way as well. Russ returned to

New York, seemingly clear on his own choice of paths forward. Meredith and Cassie sat firm until Russ had cleared the way forward for their various *News-NewYork* projects. Raymond met with his new superiors to hand off his carefully sculpted police unit and then worked with his new colleagues to learn more about the various plans. Unending detail swallowed every moment when the group was not individually at work on their existing jobs, and families.

And Meredith felt like a personal assistant to the producer-director of the Westside Elementary School's Holiday Festival, Maribelle Davis. Picking up costumes, referring hair stylists, borrowing professional make-up kits. Meredith wondered whether her self-inflicted debt to the jovial, heavy-set, massively present Mirabelle in her wide tunics and colorful tent dresses would ever be resolved.

The night before the highly touted Westside Holiday Festival, Raymond opened a beer while dinner was being prepared by Lupe and sat down with a clunk in his favorite living room lounger. Upstairs loud and heavy rhythmic bass beats flowed out of Riley's room. Raymond winced. Meredith sat down in the adjoining lounger and blew out a sigh. "One more day. After tomorrow I have to get distance from Mirabelle. She's like the Energizer Bunny—and I already have enough going on that I can't be her partner in stress. And, are you ready to be totally enthusiastic and profusely complimentary to your daughter's music folly—whatever it's going to look like?"

"Sure," he said. "But she'll have to stop that rap from blaring throughout the house. No more excuse. Oh—by the way, Tad's coming up for the show. Says he wouldn't miss it." Meredith rolled her eyes.

"He must have something more compelling than a middle school Christmas concert."

"He says he's bringing a friend," Raymond smiled wickedly.

"Oh—intrigue. Girl friend?"

Raymond shook his head. "Don't know. We'll find out. He'll

stop here first so we can go together."

When the younger half-brother arrived at the Raymond-Ogden house, with him was a familiar face. "Lola?" blurted Meredith as the couple entered the house. The striking young Latina woman smiled both mischievously, and a little embarrassed as well. The former nanny and housekeeper for the Raymonds during her college years, Lola had graduated, moved on to graduate school and finishing that, accepted a teaching job in Santa Barbara.

"Long drive to pick up a date," murmured Raymond to his brother who lived as far south of L.A. as Lola lived North.

"Geographically undesirable in Santa Barbara. Glad she moved to a Long Beach school," the young man said winking at his sibling. "Met when we came home from Kona a while ago. She was Riley-sitting while you were gone. I stayed here for the night before driving home to Irvine. She fixed a great omelet for breakfast. Hey—this is just an outing. We both wanted to see Riley do her thing."

"We'd better get going," Meredith interrupted. "Riley has been at the school for two hours and the festival starts in about an hour. The foursome trundled out the door.

"What's the news on your move from the police unit and into the private world, T.K.?" Tad asked in the car enroute to the school.

"Getting all the loose ends at the department taken care of. For the short term my long-time partner Marty Escobar will take over but the whole thing will soon change. I'm already talking with Steve Ellsworth, my new colleague at Sterner Ellsworth. We're setting up the schedule and kind of hierarchy. I'm actually finding the whole thing challenging and actually very … well … exciting. I sound like a third grader."

"Good," said Tad. "New jobs should do that."

"What about you, Meredith?" chimed Lola. Long-time house helped turned mentee of the journalist.

"Not so clear-eyed right now. I'm going to New York the week before Christmas and meeting with a couple of potential syndication companies and also with the editor of one of the big metropolitan papers that syndicates its writers. But … well, the most fruitful meeting is with one of the big more literary-type general public magazines known for its quality and in-depth writing. Think of *The Atlantic* or the *New Yorker*. Their writers are also syndicated to some major newspapers across the globe. Russ is going with me to these meetings and is also being primed with more questions by Alan and his media attorney. I hope to know more by Christmas."

"Can you handle both the TV series and a full job as a columnist?" pressed Lola.

"All to be determined," said Meredith.

Arriving at the school, the foursome joined the stream of parents and family members heading into the school auditorium. Passing through the double doors, Meredith was pulled aside by a small hand of a gnome-dressed preteen. "Missus Davis needs you right now, she says," he hissed. He grabbed her hand and pulled. Beckoning her own family into the big room, she followed the student.

Back around the side yard of the building and into the back door of the stage area, Meredith was grabbed by the shoulders by the large, firm hands of Mirabelle. "Meredith, I'm in trouble and need your calm help. Jarvis fell this morning and broke her ankle and can't come or sing in the show. Any ideas what to do?"

Meredith temped down a snarky reaction, remembering her vow to step away from the Mirabelle steam train. "Mirabelle," I'm a writer, with a full-time job and contrary to popular belief, have no real sway with the celebrities I write about. Especially in a last minute emergency on a Sunday. And I can't sing. Not a note! I'm so sorry."

The defeated look on her friend's face compelled her to reach out and hug the solid woman. She added, "You said the kids have the harmonies for that one song down well. Have them sing that. Everyone will love it. And I have to get back to my own family. I'm sorry I can't do more." She affectionately squeezed a frenetic Mirabelle's arm, turned and hurried into the auditorium.

Sliding into the hard wooden seats facing the stage, she looked at Raymond and shook her head. "Mirabelle?" he asked.

"For later. A slight change in the program today."

The lights dimmed and the curtains across the ample school stage opened to reveal Santa's workshop filled with small bodies humming and "working" at small tables, singing a familiar song or two. The story unfolded from the North Pole. Meredith nudged Raymond's arm and glanced at the couple next to him and the discreet placement of their hands clasped together. Raymond smiled.

Then with a percussive clang, on the stage, out came a colorful, confident Rudolph reindeer. Dressed in a brown leotard with antlers in her curly hair and a big red nose affixed to her own. A holiday rap song from one or another popular recording star filled the auditorium, and Rudolph began a hip-hop routine that occasionally broke into break dance moves atypical for a seven-year-old. Riley stunned her parents and fully entertained the entire audience.

"So that's what all that thumping was about," murmured Raymond.

"I helped," Lola admitted. "When you guys were in Kona we did some training."

"And she says she's going to be an astronaut," murmured Meredith.

The finale arrived with soft lighting and the entire young cast flowing in from the stage sides, all wearing lovely glittering capes, dresses or tunics. They sang shortened versions of melodic and emotional carols until the show's director stepped into the middle of the mele and, from her three-hundred-pound, gossamer tent-like dress, warbled "I'll Be Home For Christmas" in a beautiful soprano voice that soared throughout the auditorium, carrying the audience with it.

Meredith instinctively grabbed Raymond's arm and whispered, "and she wanted a 'professional.' She got the best of all possible worlds."

Raymond looked at Meredith slyly and murmured, "Is this when and where the fat lady finally sings?" Meredith elbowed him in the ribs.

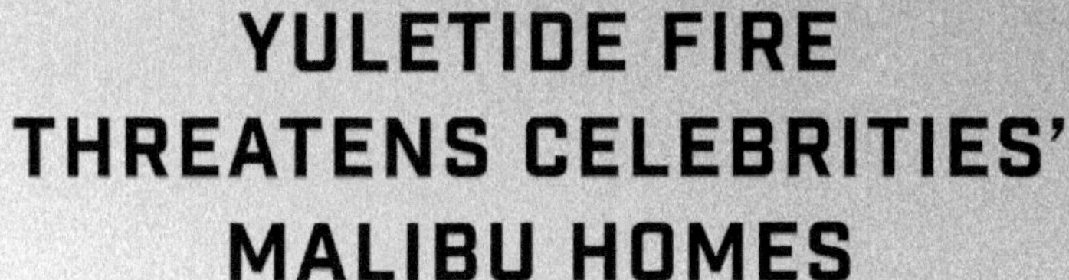

YULETIDE FIRE
THREATENS CELEBRITIES'
MALIBU HOMES

1999

Meredith decided to take Las Virgenes Road and Malibu Canyon Road over the Santa Monica Mountains from Calabasas in the west San Fernando Valley to the beach community where she lived. She'd been visiting her old friend and mentor Alan Jaymar who lived at the Sunshine Movie-TV Farm/retirement community, dropped off a Christmas bundle of goodies and gifts, and talked for a while about the new TV series contract he'd just helped negotiate for her with the CRC TV network.

As she turned on to the Pacific Coast Highway toward her home, she noticed the small beach house that her husband detective T.K. Raymond once owned—where his son Will and girlfriend lived during college and where Meredith and Raymond often spent weekends. The cottage was sold when a long-time friend of the detective—octogenarian owner and resident of a large, picturesque house a mile or so south on the beach—offered a very attractive price for Raymond to buy his larger, seductive property. The charming two-bedroom beach house found new owners as Raymond and Meredith moved their full life into the typically California coastal larger residence. There, they had grown in all ways and now filled the place with a natural and extended family.

Meredith was struck with impulsive familiarity and curiosity and pulled into the driveway of the small beach cottage as she saw a young woman placing a sign next to the building.

"For sale? Really?"

The young woman affirmed with a "yep—want to come in and see?" With no purpose but nosiness, Meredith agreed. Fifteen minutes later, she climbed into her car, thanking the real estate woman. "The addition of the bedroom and bath and family room make quite a difference," she said, really to no one in particular. Then headed home to meet the demands of the holiday season.

Christmas was always celebrated with purpose and aplomb at the Raymond-Ogden household. Busy activity was again afoot with many big and small hands and voices traditionally preparing for Christmas Eve. From the cheery robust wreath on the front door to the stockings drooping from the fireplace mantle to the seven-foot tree bearing ornaments, photos, garlands and sparkle placed by a multitude of hands, eyes and memories, the yuletide season carried a special glow.

The holidays had always been the gateway to many of life's steppingstones for Meredith Ogden and T.K. Raymond, including the formation of their own relationship and the conception of their now seven-year-old daughter Riley—a major turbulence in the solo flights of the two previously independent people. They always had reason to cheer on the yuletide. This year brought the whole actual and extended family together. Aptly so, since so many we're on the brink of new work and life paths. Much conversation, ideas and opinions were promised.

The holidays filling the Malibu beach house this year were especially fulsome. With Christmas Eve on a Friday, out-of-town celebrants arrived Thursday night or early Friday morning, expected to stay until Sunday, December 26.

Will, Raymond's thirty-seven-year-old son from an earlier marriage, wife Sophie and their nine-year-old son Kit were visiting from Seattle. Also bunking in was detective T.K.'s half-brother Tad, now thirty-four, with girlfriend Lola. Meredith's long-time colleague/friend and "adopted cousin," Ito, was also in the mix. His newest lady-friend, Julie, would join the group on Christmas Day. The village also included local holiday revelers Cassie O'Connell, Meredith's long-time colleague and pal, with Russ Talbot, Cassie's now heart-partner but for years boss to both of the women. Lola's aunt and Raymond-domestic-doyen, Lupe, directed the food and overall operation of the household.

"Ogden-Raymond Incorporated," Lola had branded the place. "Raymond-Ogden Incorporated," Will Raymond countered. "Old school," said Lola. "Male ego," said Will's wife Sophie.

Shortly after noon, Cassie and Russ arrived, bearing a half case of merlot, a large, covered pan of sweet potatoes, and assorted other gift-wrapped packages. As Lupe and Lola took the potatoes into the kitchen to incorporate with the rest of meal, and Russ found Raymond to stash the wine, Cassie found Meredith picking up Riley's room for Kit to occupy during the visit. Riley was bunking with her parents in their large master bedroom.

"Have you seen any news this morning," asked Cassie seriously.

"Fat chance," laughed Meredith. "Usually tuned into four different TV news stations, but this is vacation time. Something I should know?"

"Cassie scowled and thought for a moment. "It's probably nothing at all, but there's a fire burning across the highlands north of here, but in the mountains. The morning news said there was an alert out—that was two hours ago. I almost called but it didn't sound that threatening—yet."

Straightening up with a jolt, Meredith glanced at Cassie, then toward the stairs. "Let's check it out." Fires around Malibu even with the adjacency of the ocean were on-going concerns. The surf-side communities had suffered many times over decades as flames licked across the highway and consumed homes. Ninety fires had consumed property and homes over the past century. All seasons, all economies, no pattern. Chattering down the steps into the living room, Meredith called out to Raymond, in deep discussion with

Will and Tad. "Have you heard anything about a wildfire in the hills?"

He looked up and shook his head. "Haven't, but also haven't been very far from my duties in the kitchen and on the patio. Let me call in to the department and see what they know." Son and brother looked up, mild concern on their faces.

Sounds from TV emanated shortly from Meredith's small alcove office as she and Cassie channel-jumped looking for news of a fire near Malibu. Soon one droning news voice after another was telling a story. The assembled household flowed into the office doorway. "Prevailing winds, fast moving across the hills, keeping a close eye on it … warning residents just in case … " Cassie repeated for the benefit of those listening nearby.

Then Raymond interrupted, edging his way through the throng and into the center of the small room. "Dispatcher at work says department is beefing up support personnel, working very tight with the fire folks. They're more than mildly worried about this one. Wind direction, dryness of the terrain. Thinking to alert residents very soon."

"What does that mean?" asked ten-year-old Kit, eyes wide in terror.

"He's terrified of surprises," said Sophie. "We don't know why."

"It's not a bad trait," murmured Raymond, loping through the house and out the front door, grabbing a pair of binoculars that resided permanently on a table inside. From the front patio he sprang up to a low side-wall along the steps and focused the glasses on the northern horizon. Scanning the view for a few minutes, he stepped back down to face the group watching him from the door. "Smoke rising above the hills. I don't see any red, glow or flames, but … " At that moment the distant whine of emergency sirens pierced the air, first at a distance but obviously growing closer. He ushered the throng back into the house. Better to not stress-watch, he figured. Instinctively but discreetly, he knew what would have to happen.

"Nothing to worry about yet," he said with assurance. "Back to work." He waved everyone toward the center of the house from where they had been when the rumor started about a fire. But he grabbed Meredith subtly by the hand and took her with him into the garage. "This isn't good. And it won't go well. I think we need to plan an alternative."

Her face fell, disappointment etched clearly. "I'm sorry," he said sincerely. "I know you wanted this to be a rare, big warm family gathering. The first ever. It doesn't mean that we can't still celebrate together, but … "

"Well," she grimaced. "It isn't like we don't know how to make the best of emergencies." Raymond noticed she was girding back to her usual straight shouldered, head-held-high verve. Raymond's phone beeped in his pocket. He turned away to press it to his ear. A few grunts, "uh-huhs" and a "thanks" and he turned back, apologetically.

"Highway patrol is going to block off Pac Coast highway several miles north. Possibly—eventually—down this way, eventually, as well, to leave a route for emergency vehicles and people."

"Evacuating residents?"

He looked away. "Maybe, probably." Cassie pushed open the door and announced, "Gloria is on the phone, Meredith. Wants to talk to you." She handed her friend the mobile. "I told her what was going on," simmered Cassie. I thought she should know."

Meredith's oldest friend, former roommate, and frequent wing-woman, Gloria Masner, was conveniently married to Raymond's former fraternity brother and long-time golf buddy and pal. They, too, were part of the extended family of friends that formed the network of love and support.

"They haven't declared evacuation time yet," Meredith moaned.

"Bring that tribe over here," commanded Gloria, who lived in a large mansion inland in a near-legendary gated-housing community.

"I wouldn't do that to you. You have no idea how huge this gang is. Think *Cheaper By the Dozen*," whimpered Meredith.

"Meredith," commanded Gloria. "We're by ourselves tonight—just George and I and Trey. All the holiday falderal for us was over yesterday. I have five bedrooms and a pool house. You know we can accommodate this. Bring it all—food, presents … kids … "

"Do you have a tree?" whimpered Meredith, tears threatening—not only from her own disappointment but appreciation toward her friend.

"Of course we do. You know that. You were here two weeks ago. We're always the brightest bulb on Christmas! And Trey will love it," she said referring to their adopted son, considered a "cousin" to Riley.

"Ok," simpered Meredith. Raymond grasped the phone away and spoke into it, holding up a "wait here" finger to both Cassie and Meredith. As he clicked off, handing the instrument back to Meredith, he said, "we have some fast planning to do. But, we have lots of warm bodies to get the job done and moved over to Holmby Hills." He pulled Cassie into the garage, closed the door behind her and took a pen from his shirt pocket. He twisted around to reach inside the car and extract a small notebook kept in the door pocket. The three leaned against the car and began to strategize.

Ten minutes later, they calmly left the garage and called the various visitors together in the living room. "We're spending Christmas Eve and Morning at a luxurious resort in Holmby Hills. It's private but wow, the real deal. The only catch is that we have to make the thirty-minute drive there—cars loaded—very soon. And we'll be taking all the cars."

"Evacuating because of the fire?" ventured Will, a sly confident half-grin on his face. Raymond shrugged and Meredith stepped up with her list and began the count down. More sirens clanged by the house, encouraging the group to hustle.

"Sophie, repack all your things including the presents and put them in your car. Tad and Lola the same … "

"And Tad," Raymond jumped in, "once you have your belongings in YOUR car, can you and Will—my two computer scientists—please help me pack up the necessary technology—computers CPU'S, cables, phones and cords and put them in my car."

"Lola," Meredith stepped in, "will you please help Lupe pack up some things for a couple of days, then with Sophie and Ito's help, pack up the food. You know where the extra storage containers are, but lots of things are already in carrying containers."

Raymond: "Russ, will you and Cassie help Meredith figure out what files and paperwork to bring—like CDs and well … figure it out. Equipment like cameras and recorders … "

"I'll also be packing us up," Meredith reported, "plus all extra presents and a few other items. And Paco."

"I can pack up Paco," said Lola, "with Riley's help. Kit can help us with whatever else we think should go." Then the assembled group only seemed to stare.

"Go now," snapped Cassie and all hustled off to their respective tasks. Will sidled over to Raymond and quietly said, "Go take care of your house and family. Tad and I can handle the tech. Honest. We pretty much know what to do." Raymond blinked and moved toward the garage to clean out the car and grab a couple of overnight cases. Then swept up the stairs to open the safe and collect personal papers and valuable jewelry kept there.

As cars were stuffed with suitcases, bags and presents, and packing up was hastily completed within the house, smoke was wafting down Pacific Coast Highway. The wispy grey soot clouds were now less than three miles north of the residential enclave where the Raymond home was located. Several neighbors filed out of their homes, loading up vehicles and driving away.

Lola had sent Riley into the garage for the soft screened pet holder and kept it out of sight until Lola, herself, reached up to the top of the refrigerator, holding a treat, and lured Paco into her arms.

The seventeen-year-old feline gave no complaint as she eased him into the holder and zipped it up. Wise beyond what was expected of a cat who spent most of his years atop the refrigerator, he knew better than to resist. He, in his carrier, along with a bag of cat food cans, and full litter box was placed into the back trunk of the SUV.

"Checked dispatch a few minutes ago," Raymond murmured to Meredith as they stuffed their own emergency clothing and toiletries into duffle bags. "Evacuation notices going out in a few minutes to all residents along the coast. We'll be seeing someone soon with bullhorns and knocking on doors.

In less than a half hour later, Meredith handed out photocopied maps of the route to Gloria's house, and the first four cars of their caravan set out from the Malibu residence. They would just beat a burgeoning line of automobiles exiting the area expected as the air became more dense with smoke tendrils and a slight glow could be seen north in the distance above the hills.

Riley had been secured in the back seat of Tad's car, along with Lupe, Lola in the front. The curly-haired child reached out to Meredith. " … Mom … will you come too?" Fear and anxiety on the small face, eyes briming with tears. The stress from the past hour had captured the youngsters' emotions as well as the adults'. "And Paco, will he come?" pressed Riley.

Meredith patted the translucent cheek. "We're right behind you, honey. You'll see us and Paco before you get settled at Aunt Gloria's." Tears ran down the child's face. And her own nearly obliterated her mother's vision as well.

Meredith and Raymond then efficiently made the rounds to check windows, electrical switches, water controls and other important elements of the house, making sure all complied with known recommendations for safety evacuation. And sealing off of the house to damage. On the last sweep through the rooms, Meredith grabbed the small worn teddy bear from Riley's bed. Raymond, the wedding photo of himself and Meredith and the fat photo album on a bottom shelf of the bookcase. His last stop was the hidden, locked gun safe in the kitchen. He retrieved his pistol and pushed it into his carryall along with a box of ammunition. Overnight duffels, cat, work materials, valuables and personal papers stowed, they had quickly closed and locked the doors before climbing into their cars, glancing hastily back with some sadness and trepidation, at the house that was their home. Meredith stared at the roadway ahead, afraid to look back and acknowledge the threat.

Although they left the Malibu house only a scant ten minutes after the early family caravan, Meredith and Raymond did not pull up to the Masner's estate for a full hour after the earlier group arrived. Traffic out of the Malibu area, chased by the ominous smoke clouds and imagined as well as a few real fire sparks had increased quickly and residents were leaving more rapidly.

As the couple unloaded the cars, friends Gloria and George rushed out to welcome them. The sturdily built host, his nearly bald head bobbing in action, his dancing eyes quickly identified items he could help take into the house. Gloria embraced Meredith who worked hard not to seem frazzled and shaken. Her old friend whispered in her ear, "It's going to okay. Honest. You know, we always manage to skirt disaster!"

In her crisp no-nonsense commands, Gloria directed Raymond, Meredith and Riley—and Paco—to the "large" guest suite with its massive canopied king-sized bed and pull-out sofa, plus a full decorous bathroom. Will and Sophie, another sizeable guest suite, Tad and Lola, the pool house, a self-contained cottage, Lupe, the nearly stand-alone quarters usually occupied by their own house manager, Margaret, away visiting family for the holidays. Ito took the office/library with its leather pull-out, and the boys—Kit and Trey—doubled up in Trey's room. When Cassie and Russ insisted on returning to their own place in Manhattan Beach, Gloria refused the idea and put them in the atrium. Only the kitchen, living room, office and laundry room were left without a sleeping body tucked in to them.

"You always wanted to be an innkeeper," Raymond mused

toward his friend George. "But where's the golf course?"

"What do these people do that required so much guest space?" Murmured Tad to Lola.

"They're very rich and help out friends in need," she snickered.

The household settled in for the Christmas Eve celebration. Presents had been transported and rearranged under the Masner's tree, stocking hung from a storybook fireplace mantel. Pans, containers and pots of food were being prepared in the near-commercial kitchen by Ito, Lupe and Lola with Meredith, Sophie and Cassie setting up the banquet table. All worked with a hyper energy that helped stave off anxiety.

A TV located in the library was kept turned on, low level audio, to monitor the fire news. From time to time someone compulsively peered in at the screen, noting the fire and its threat to the community from where they had exited. The pulsating wish was to pass Christmas without a tragedy.

Riley, Trey, and Kit were in front of another television watching a Christmas movie. And as Riley often said, "My dad and his friends just like to smoke cigars and drink beer." Behaviors most of them only enjoyed on the rare occasion when they were together without business or golf. Occasions like Christmas Eve when they also played a game or two of pool—or helped set up a Christmas meal.

And all worked to avoid focusing on the news, fixating on the status of the fire in Malibu. "We won't be doing that," Meredith announced with great passion. "We're here. It's Christmas Eve and we're all together. Can we make the specialness of that the center of focus, not the tragic chaos going on at the coast? There's not a thing we can do about it now, so let's be here instead." The fiery mayhem was pushed aside—mostly—for the night of revelry, gift opening, cocoa and brandy sipping and even a couple of carols sung—badly. Stories were shared. And when the lights flickered out for the night throughout the large domicile, most likely everyone was thinking about the fire and the fate of the house on the bluff overlooking the ocean. Even Paco wondered if his beloved refrigerator still stood. Meanwhile, he curled tightly against the back of Riley, who everyone hoped was dreaming of Santa and sugarplums.

Quietly, discreetly, Gloria Masner turned on the TV live news—without sound—in her and George's bedroom and saw no change in the fire's path. No homes were burned along Malibu's coast. At least not yet. She switched off the news and said nothing to anyone else.

"A nice Christmas Eve in any case," whispered Raymond into Meredith's ear as they lay resting against one another in the large ornate guestroom. "I hope you're doing as well as you seemed during the evening."

"None of our thoughts was very far away from Malibu," she whispered back to him. "But a big whopping Christmas is so much for the kids, and it wasn't fair to burden them with the hazards of reality this year." Her dreams were not of sugarplums but flames and sirens.

Christmas Day dawned with crisp lovely weather on the Masner household. After a creative breakfast conjured mostly by Ito and served buffet style, Tad and Lola took the three children off to the pedal boats in Echo Park, an urban oasis east of Hancock Park and one of the few attractions open on the holiday.

As soon as the youngsters left the premises, the large TV in the family room was turned to news. The whipped-up fire threatening the community of Malibu was being held in abeyance just before reaching the Highway and was now under control enough for residents, tucked into alternative housing, to take a few optimistic breaths with more hope than twelve hours earlier.

"Still a waiting game," Raymond reported after calling into his office dispatcher. "But possibly fully controlled in a few hours."

Then the adults grouped together under the roof of the pool patio, sipping on beer, brandy, tea and assorted soft drinks to catch up without the tinkle of Christmas goings-on. Raymond reported his last day in the Special Profile unit of the Police Department would be the next Friday, December 31. "Meredith and I are taking a two-week cruise starting two days later before I start up with my new gig." The gig was as a legal representative for a major creative management firm that handled talent of all types, mostly theatrical. "I'm a fixer," joked Raymond.

"Meredith?" goaded Gloria, fully aware that a team of television producers, with Meredith, would be writing and producing a new TV series featuring a character who mirrored Meredith's decades long role as Hollywood journalist. "They think all my work involves murders, threats, scams … "

"Doesn't it?" teased Russ, her former boss, recently retired, at the media syndicate which was now sold and disbanded. "But," he continued, "Meredith'll be doing monthly articles for an as-yet-undisclosed national magazine that will be syndicating those to her existing newspapers."

"No more daily deadlines?" asked George Masner.

Meredith shook her head. "And with the sale of the media syndicate," she quickly added, "Cassie will be the on-site producer for the new series I'm working on."

Cassie smiled self-consciously, then added, "And Ito will join the production staff at the network as the financial officer." The slender Japanese man blushed then tinkered with his glasses. The young slender, petite, blonde lady next to him, Julie, who joined the crowd that morning, looked on with some surprise but clearly from outside the closely knit family circle.

Russ looked away with a grin. "I feel lazy just retiring," he said, "and moving here to the west coast to golf."

"We know how long that'll last," mused Raymond. Cassie let out a loud guffaw.

"But what of Sonia," Gloria asked of the decades-long editorial assistant and now columnist with Meredith at *News—New York*.

"She's fine," Meredith answered. "Several years ago, she and her husband, Art, bought a small weekly shopper newspaper in the eastern San Fernando Valley where they live. She wrote and edited the stories. Art has two sons from a previous marriage, and she has one. One of each took over the Weekly some time ago, increased it to twice a week a couple of years ago and she is still the editor. That's continued as the circulation and advertising has grown, so they're all busy. She'll still give me one day a week for research and admin if I need it. We'll see how it goes."

All eyes turned toward Gloria and George. "Hey," the elegant brunette said with a wave of her well-manicured hand. "Same old, same old—George pushes the rock and rock stars up the hill with his music agency and I'm still helping older folks with their trusts and wills. And entertaining and harboring refugees from Malibu."

Raymond slipped out of his seat to check with his dispatcher about the fire's status. "About the same, I think we'll need to figure out what and where tonight will happen. We can't ask these lovely hosts to provide dinner or another night of free lodging," he reported.

"Nuts with that," barked George. "There must be some restaurants open on Christmas Day. We'll go out to dinner and the rooms are already messed up. Tomorrow's only Sunday and Margaret—and her scour and buff cleaning troops—will be back on Monday. No harm, no foul."

"And," smiled Gloria, "it's such a pleasure having a full house of loving friends. Different from the usual business guests."

"Let's see what happens next," suggested Meredith. "If we can go home, we should. Otherwise, well, we may have no choice." Quiet ensued for a few moments, everyone sipping at their beverage of choice. Then Meredith spoke up with levity. "I've told there are some advantages to losing your home. I recall an interview with Angela Lansbury a few years back in the 1970 Malibu fire. Her home was destroyed. But the next day, she was on the set of the movie she was starring in, and accepted a media interview. When the reporter asked her what it was like to lose a long-time home and all the belongings in it, she came right back with something like, 'At my age, what woman wouldn't be happy to have a good reason to start over!'"

"You're not old enough to make that claim," sniffed Cassie. Meredith shrugged.

"Maybe it's not about chronologic age but maturity," she whimpered. "And I'm not mature enough to be that existential."

"Oh, for goodness' sake," growled Will. "I'm challenging everyone here to a game of pool." He rose, and the rest of the group followed along to the pool table. Soon, Ito, his friend Julie, Sophie, and Cassie were deep in a poker melee. Others played Monopoly. Lupe puttered around the kitchen with Gloria accompanying her.

"No, I'm not going to play strip poker!" barked Cassie at one point.

Over the pool table when just the two were parrying, Will commented, "It's kind of sad with Grandma gone now. We used to spend the holidays with her in Newport Beach." Then he turned and said to Raymond, "I'm glad I have had a chance to spend time with Tad. I'd still like to know more about you two and why it took you so long to meet one another."

Raymond lined up a shot, struck it, watching the small colorful balls scatter across the table. "That's for another time. It's a long tough story and I will tell it to you—just not right here, right now."

Will snuffed out a groan of frustration. "Never enough time, dad. I feel like I need to know. I'm older than he is!" The young man lined up his own shot, took it.

"You do need to understand, I agree," Raymond said. "You're staying with us another couple of days—hoping we can get back home and settle in. Wherever we are the next couple of days, you and I will take some time to ourselves, and you'll get the whole story. I promise."

"Yeah, I'm older than my uncle, and my son Kit is also a year older than his own aunt, Riley. What an odd family we have."

Lunch was snacks from the previous day's dinner. The swan boat paddlers had enjoyed hot dogs from a stand near Echo Lake and returned about three o'clock. Naps seemed to beckon to most of the household and George found a nearby French restaurant that was open and could handle the whole group for dinner. Throughout the day, TV news was switched on and off as updates to the Malibu fire were sought. Mostly, the word was "status—the same." Holding the inferno away from the beach residential areas. "Residents not allowed back into the area." Meredith ground her teeth in frustration without a good picture of the situation at their house. Her hands were sore from clenching them. Waiting was not her strong suit.

At one point, she stared out a kitchen window, her face folded into an anxious glower. Lupe walked up, hands on her wide hips, and scolded, "Stop this! Go out and do something! Standing around here in your state helps no one—and certainly not you!" Raymond often called Lupe "El Générale" for a good reason. Meredith quietly slipped upstairs, put on her athletic shoes—the only other pair she brought—and discreetly left the house for a long run through the rows of large properties and houses. Frightening visions of her neighborhood and home left in embers plagued her thoughts although she worked hard to dismiss them.

As the day waned, Ito, Russ and Cassie suggested they return to their own L.A. area residences. Even Tadd and Lola proposed they return to their respective homes an hour and fifteen minutes south, but Gloria would hear none of it. And George added his jovial perspective, "Oh hell, I told you before, you've already messed up the rooms. Take advantage of the attention lavished on you for another night. We're enjoying this and Gloria is reveling. Don't burst her balloon."

They didn't. But that evening, the nearby French restaurant hadn't seen that much chatter, wine orders or appreciative tips for working a holiday, when the entourage finally traipsed out the door.

And the TV was on as soon as the first person entered the Masner home. Raymond put in his own call to his source and returned with, "Nearly there. The blaze is about eighty percent contained, expected to be out of threat category by midnight. But no one is encouraging residents to return. So, it'll probably be tomorrow morning before we hear an 'all clear to go home.' Assuming there's not a flareup or … "

"You just want to smoke some more cigars and drink more … brandy … with George," Meredith snickered, wagging her head toward Riley who had minted the comment a couple of years before. Raymond nodded in agreement.

Watching the 1946 traditional Christmas film *It's a Wonderful Life*, Trey and Kit first peeled off to their beds. Riley, yawning, took the same journey a few minutes later. Various guests followed gradually one by one until Raymond was the only person left on the main floor. He turned off the set then checked in with his dispatcher one more time. Disheartened that the status of the fire was unchanged, and the winds were picking up, he sighed and turned off the last of the lights, making his way up to the suite where his two beloved women—and one okay cat—were already sound asleep.

"Guess what Santa brought us a day late?" Meredith whispered to a snoozing Riley as the sun was just arising. The small girl screwed up her face in wake-up mode and opened one eye.

"But Santa already came night before last," she whimpered.

"No, he bought us a special delivery last night. It wasn't ready yet before then."

The little girl sat up, rubbed her eyes, and yawned. "What?"

"He brought us our home back—safe from the fire. It's all there."

"Oh," said Riley, looking up blandly at her mother.

"Well, get up and have some breakfast with us. We can go home today."

"Oh," said the girl.

The exodus from the Masner estate took place quickly once breakfast was cleaned up. Each room occupant took responsibility for cleaning up their own leftovers. Linens stripped, bathrooms tidied, and whatever else needed picking up. Meredith mused that it took only about twenty minutes at the Malibu house to evacuate in full, and much more than that to pack up from the Masner's home. Cassie and Russ headed to their own home in Manhattan Beach. Ito and his friend Julie to Venice Beach, Tad and Lola to Irvine. The three Raymond cars set out with Will, Sophie, and Kit in one car; Meredith, Riley, and Paco in another; and Raymond and Lupe in the third one.

Air kisses were tossed between Gloria Masner and Meredith, with the latter wondering how in the world she could ever thank her friend for the hospitality—and the rescue.

Once back to the house on the beach, Meredith felt a deep sense of relief that the place still stood, looking as welcoming as it had before they exited. The family took a deep tour of the place to see what detritus was left after the fire was quelled. Stale air still hovered after the blaze was announced to be contained and residents were allowed to return to their homes. Fortunately for the Raymonds, the actual flare-ups had been stopped several miles north, but the soot and dust covered much of the landscape and gave some challenge to breathing.

The family, reorganized back in the house, and life settled some after the chaotic escape two days before, Raymond and Will left for a walk on the beach and the promised discussion about the discovery of Raymond's half-brother Tad.

Meredith, Sophie, and Lupe pulled together a simple meal. Kit and Riley were playing a game in the family room. Meredith finally sat down with a cup of tea and thumbed through the local Sunday paper. She was deep in thought about "changes." There were so many on the horizon, propelling her into a different mental picture of the future.

After the dinner was finished, Will's family and Riley were asleep, Lupe back in her own quarters and Paco settled on the refrigerator until the lights were out when he would move into Riley's room.

Perched on a stool at the kitchen island, Meredith set down her teacup, and took a deep breath. "Raymond," she spoke up in her serious forthright manner. "I'd like to talk about some things."

Oh, oh, he thought.

She shook her head, "Don't look so stricken," she laughed. He joined her at the kitchen island. "What a wild and exciting life we have here in this big house," Meredith started. "It's everything we've needed for the past ten years. It's housed everything from new life, the essence of Hollywood news and gossip, welcoming to a new brother, and has been the center of hundreds of strategy sessions and decision negotiations." She blew out a brisk "Whew." Raymond's mind went into hyper drive with memories of the discussion sessions, the work, the debates, the love, love-making, and the challenges.

"And you've been the world's most gracious host and patriarch—and partner."

Raymond shuddered at the words, wondering what was next. "Are you firing me?" he asked, irony lacing his words. Meredith laughed and shook her head.

"I've been a ring master, a clown, a drama conductor, boss and a dance captain." She continued, chuckling. He regarded her with deep intensity, working to figure out where the conversation was going.

"The past three days has been … well, instructional. Incited way too much concern and responsibility—even to the house itself. Too much stress, more than my meager shoulders can carry. We don't need all the facilities and room now—and certainly not in the future. There's no staff arriving daily, no tiny toddler any longer. My thoughts always go back to the simplicity of the Brentwood condo where we first spent our time together—and spending weekends of quiet and escape in your great little beach cottage. Havens, our own nests. I'm tired of the circus. Conducting the chaos and managing the tent city."

"I'm not sure where this is going," he puzzled to her.

"A few days ago, I was driving home from Calabasas and as I drove by the old beach house, I saw it was for sale and stopped in to look. The owners added another bedroom and family room. I was reminded of how nice and simple things were at that charming beach house. Garage for two, nice master bedroom and bath, one office-guest room, now, one small child's room, a small place, nice deck out to the sand. Kitchen has been updated some. And there's a great refrigerator overlooking it all—for Paco."

Raymond looked at her with questions etched across his face.

"Next year is a new Millenium. Raymond, I'd really like to shed some of the melee and superstructure—and have the beach cottage be our New Year's present to ourselves. What do you think?"

ABOUT THE AUTHOR

Penny Pence Smith was "legwoman" (assistant) to a famous Hollywood gossip columnist, a role that grew into a field correspond and Los Angeles Bureau Manager covering the entertainment industry for the *New York Time Special Features Syndicate,* and later correspondent for the *Hollywood Reporter.* Her journalism career began at age 14 as a reporter for her local Southern California daily newspaper. With a Ph.D. in Communication Research she has consulted to high tech, health care, public health and finance companies and taught journalism and communication at UNC Chapel Hill and Hawaii Pacific University. Her *Under a Maui Sun* and *Reflections of Kauai* were best-selling tourism books in Hawaii where she lives with her husband.

Check Penny's Author Page on BookBub and Goodreads for news about future Meredith Ogden adventures and other books: pennystories.wix site.com/penny-smith-books.